THE

AMERICAN

VISITORS

First edition published in 2024
© Copyright 2024
Allison Osborne

The right of Allison Osborne to be identified as the author of this work has been asserted by her in accordance with the Copyright, Designs and Patents Act 1998.

All rights reserved. No reproduction, copy or transmission of this publication may be made without express prior written permission. No paragraph of this publication may be reproduced, copied or transmitted except with express prior written permission or in accordance with the provisions of the Copyright Act 1956 (as amended). Any person who commits any unauthorised act in relation to this publication may be liable to criminal prosecution and civil claims for damage.

All characters appearing in this work are fictitious. Any resemblance to real persons, living or dead, is purely coincidental. The opinions expressed herein are those of the author and not of Orange Pip Books.

Paperback ISBN: 978-1-80424-449-4
ePub ISBN: 978-1-80424-450-0
PDF ISBN: 978-1-80424-451-7

Published by Orange Pip Books
335 Princess Park Manor, Royal Drive,
London, N11 3GX
www.orangepipbooks.com

HOLMES & CO. MYSTERIES

COLLECTION ONE
THE INTRODUCTION OF HOLMES & CO

A STUDY IN VICTORY RED
THE CIRCLE CODE CONUNDRUM
THE IMPOSSIBLE MURDERER
THE HAPPY FAMILY FACADE
THE RED ROVER SOCIETY
THE DETECTIVE'S NEMESIS

COLLECTION TWO
THE ADVENTURES OF HOLMES & CO

THE HIDDEN CASE
THE MISSING TWO
THE AMERICAN VISITORS

The Press, Watson, is a most valuable institution, if you only know how to use it.

-Sherlock Holmes, *The Adventure of the Six Napoleons*

Chapter I
A Visit to The Ritz

Irene Holmes shoved the last of her bacon sandwich into her mouth and attempted to ignore the silly conversation happening in the living room of 221b Baker Street. She was tucked up in her chair, staring at the logs in the fireplace while Miss Hudson and Doctor Joe Watson yammered on from the other seats.

"It is uncanny," Joe said, handing a magazine back to Miss Hudson.

"It's downright spooky."

Irene rolled her eyes. "It is not unheard of that two people look similar."

"True," Joe agreed. "But even you have to admit, this is a bit odd."

She spun in her chair and grabbed the magazine from Miss Hudson. Actress Kathleen Carrington graced the cover, clutching the chest of her co-star Don Radcliffe in promotion for their new film 'The Thief At Midnight'.

According to Joe and Miss Hudson, the actress bore a striking resemblance to Irene, right down to the dark hair, almond eyes and pouty bottom lip.

"Perhaps we do appear alike," Irene said, if only to entertain their conversation. "But my eyebrows have never – and will never – be so *thin*. Not to mention that that shade of lipstick would wash me out completely."

"You know," Miss Hudson began, "it wouldn't hurt to try a different shade now and then."

Irene tossed the magazine on the table, unwilling to get into a discussion about makeup. Luckily, she was saved by quick, light footsteps ascending the stairs.

"Perhaps we'll see if Eddy believes in this foolishness."

Isla, the West Highland Terrier, barked from her place under the couch. She rushed to the door as DI Lestrade entered the flat, a magazine in his hand. "Good morning, all."

"Morning, Love." Miss Hudson stood, inviting him to sit. "I'll go put on a fresh pot. Oh! You've got the same issue we do. Doesn't our Irene look *just* like Miss Carrington?"

Eddy stooped to pet the dog, letting out a deep laugh. "I thought the same thing! Funny enough—"

"That's why you're here." Irene climbed off the chair and kicked her feet, loosening the legs of her pyjamas stuck around her calves. She circled the poor man, Isla following along. "You're on duty. Two coffees in already. A new case, with which you require my help. No murders involved. And—" She stooped and plucked two ginger cat hairs from his trousers. "You were at Thom's last night."

"Correct in all ways. The case, if you can call it that, is most —"

"Exciting? To whom – the common folk or me? Because, I can assure you, what you and the rest of London find exhilarating, I find mundane at best."

Eddy laughed as he settled on the couch across from Joe. "You know, just when I think you've worked on your manners, you remind me again that you are most certainly a Holmes."

Joe cleared a spot for the tea tray Miss Hudson carried into the room.

"I do try," he said without looking up. "It's working, I assure you. Though, who would our Irene be without a few slip-ups every so often?"

"Or a good scowl on her face."

Both men chuckled as the landlady dished out the tea.

Irene attempted to keep her face from giving them the satisfaction of seeing the aforementioned scowl, pursing her lips instead. Though her friends teased her, she knew they'd never actually insult her, so she played along.

"Are you two finished?" She scoffed without an ounce of annoyed gusto. "I'd like to hear about this case."

"So you *are* interested." Eddy grabbed a biscuit.

Irene sat in her chair, back straight, attentive as ever. "Of course I am. Anything that makes you this giddy intrigues me."

"Well, then. As we all know, Miss Carrington and Mr Radcliffe are in town for the premiere—"

"Yes, yes," Irene waved her hand. "Are they in danger?"

"We're not sure."

"Who is 'we'? Goodness, Eddy, you should know by now how to relay a case to me."

Joe groaned from his chair while the detective huffed at her.

"Would you like another biscuit? You're quite snappy this morning."

She glared at him, but reached out to grab one.

"As I was saying, there are film posters around the city, but a handful have been vandalised. Crossed out with red paint, mostly. A few of them have 'murderer' and 'thief' written on them."

Joe grunted. "I saw one of them, but simply thought it clever propaganda for the picture."

"Not so, unfortunately. Miss Carrington's agent, Kipp Barton, is second cousins with Mr Beauchamp from that dog case we worked last year. Beauchamp told him about you and said if there was any trouble, you would help out in an instance."

Irene slumped in the chair and didn't even attempt to hide her sarcasm. "How kind."

"They are offering a hefty sum for a security check of the theatre and the hotel they are staying at, and an investigation into the poster vandal. It's not a matter that Scotland Yard wants to handle, at least not yet. So, I'm bringing it to you."

She stayed in a puddle on the cushion and picked at her thumbnail, excitement deflated. "They want me to catch a vandal?"

"If possible, yes," Eddy said, helping himself to another biscuit. "And to insure everything is safe or, at the very least, offer any insight."

Irene had slipped too far down the chair, causing her shirt to bunch at her waistline. She adjusted herself and sat straighter, but not by much. "Where are they staying?"

"The Ritz."

Miss Hudson gasped. "Oh, Irene. You *must*."

From his chair, Joe chimed in as well. "I wouldn't mind seeing inside The Ritz."

"The suites, no less," Eddy emphasised. "Both actors are staying in one-bedrooms larger than most houses I've been in."

The three of them eagerly looked to Irene. In truth, she had been intrigued from the moment Eddy sat down, as he had become quite decent at bringing her interesting cases. Of course, she couldn't let on, as her friends would all get cheeky.

Instead, she picked at a fluff on her trousers. "Did they collect the vandalised posters?"

"They did. And noted the locations every one came from."

Irene stewed for a minute, thinking. Finally, as they all looked at each other in frustrated annoyance, she stood, clasping her hands together.

"We will view the posters and take a turn about the hotel and the venue."

"Jolly good," Eddy exclaimed. "I thought you'd be harder to convince."

She swiped another biscuit and admitted, "Perhaps a part of me is curious as to what is inside The Ritz as well."

The DI stood and gave her a sly smile. "I will see you both in the lobby of the hotel at one pm. Simply give the doorman my name and tell him you are aiding in an investigation."

"You've made arrangements for us as if we'd already said yes?"

"I knew you'd say yes to this case. It was just a matter of how long I needed to convince you. Ta-ta, see you in a few hours!"

Eddy gave her a wink, kissed Miss Hudson on the cheek, and dashed out of the flat.

"I suppose I'll dig out my finest shirt." Joe stood to leave, aiming for his upstairs bedroom. "And you surely must spritz that expensive perfume you stole from that school girl a few weeks back."

Irene sighed, other things on her mind than finery. "Be prepared for American accents, Joe. Hopefully, they are not too jarring."

"They are film stars. They're trained to be coherent."

"Only if they're following scripts."

"It will all be fine. And exciting. It's not every day that regular people like us get to meet famous film stars. And at The Ritz, no less!"

Irene waved him off. "Go upstairs. You're at risk of making me excited."

Her partner threw her a grin and continued to his room.

* * * * *

As Irene parked the '34 Vauxhall in front of the large hotel, her brow furrowed in concern. More than a dozen people – a mixture of men and women – huddled around the grand front door.

Two constables milled about, keeping an eye on the group.

Even as Irene and Joe approached, the people all watched the door. But then, suddenly, one of the women turned and gasped at Irene, causing a few more to turn their heads. Just as quickly, however, the same woman mumbled something and they all turned around again.

Irene pushed past them.

A constable halted her as she approached the door.

"I'm Irene Holmes. We're here to meet with DI Lestrade."

The crowd grew closer, listening.

Joe stepped up behind her, creating some space between her and the busybodies.

"Ah, yes," the man nodded. "Go right on in."

As she entered the building, she felt a flutter of excitement. This is only a hotel, nothing more. Sure, the place had a rich history and a well-known air of elegance, but it was still just walls and furniture.

Of course, the lobby immediately contradicted these thoughts. The plush carpet leading up to the curved dark wood desk was freshly cleaned, every marble and gold surface polished to a reflective shine.

"Where's Lestrade?" Joe craned his neck.

"Oh, if he's left us to greet these Americans alone, I will—"

Joe hooked his arm in hers. "Let's not get ahead of ourselves. He's probably still upstairs."

The pair forwent the lift, opting to take the carpeted stairs to the fourth floor.

Even the upper hallways were grand and lush. It was eerily quiet as the carpet muffled their footsteps.

As if on cue, Eddy popped out of a large suite at the end of the hall. "Welcome! So sorry, I meant to be downstairs to greet you, but was chatting with Mr. Barton. Mr. Radcliffe and Miss Carrington are in the dining room, so we've free rein of their suites."

Eddy had dolled himself up for this investigation. Not one hair was out of place; his suit pressed pressed to perfection. Irene was tempted to tease him about looking as spiffy as his partner, DI Thom Gregory, but kept her mouth shut.

If she could get most of her investigating and deducing done before the actors returned from their lunch, then the less she'd have to speak with them. Or, at the very least, narrow down her questions.

"Are they staying together?"

"No," Eddy said. "This is Mr. Radcliffe's suite, as we thought it less of an imposition than bothering Miss Carrington in hers. You can do all your sniffing around and take a look at the posters. If there is anything further needed, we will move to one of the lower-floor meeting rooms."

The slight lift in his voice told Irene that a part of him was eager to use those rooms at some point during this investigation.

They entered a grand living space of plush, clean furniture with intricate detailing. Vases and china sat in cabinets, and a fully stocked bar cart was tucked in the corner. There was a small dining table near a large window overlooking London. Irene made a mental note to glance out of it at some point. The room was pointed north, toward Baker Street. It was highly doubtful her flat would be visible from here, but she still felt the urge to gaze outside; to look at her city though a different lens.

A paunchy man with a sweaty brow and a comb-over not-so-patiently waited to be noticed. He finally stepped forward, extending his hand.

"Mr. and Mrs. Homes, thank you so much for meeting with us. You come highly recommended by Mr. Beauchamp."

His American accent had a New York twang to it and, though he looked a bit nervous, his pressed suit, small keen eyes and broad shoulders belonged to a businessman used to schmoozing Hollywood executives.

Irene gritted her teeth.

"We will be as quick and through as we can." She grasped his clammy hand. Then, she spotted the pile of posters on the coffee table. "We will take a quick turn about the room, then do the same for Miss Carrington's suite. In the meantime, please spread those posters out on the dining table. Come, Joe."

Mr. Barton only stuttered once before speaking. "Do you have any questions for me?"

"Of course. But I'm not sure which ones until I know more. The posters, please."

As Irene turned away, she saw Eddy grab the man's attention, probably attempting to explain her behaviour.

Unfazed, she headed into the small bedroom attached to the main sitting area. It was the size of their living area at Baker Street and smelled of expensive cologne. Irene, more a fan of fresh food scents – and whatever cologne Joe used – thought of an American office setting as she inhaled.

Above the dresser was a rather large mirror. She glanced at herself and Joe as they passed. While both did their best to look posh, there was a certain roughness about them. The pair had also unintentionally matched their outfits, as was becoming habit: brown vest on Joe to go along with her trousers, and a short-sleeve shirt on them both.

So far, there was nothing out of the ordinary; just a bedroom of a man with expensive taste visiting from America. The closet door was ajar, fine suits peeking out. Meanwhile, the bed behind them was freshly made and stood twice the height and width of hers. Irene poked at the plush coverings, then twirled around and fell backwards, arms outstretched.

"Oh, Joe, I would pay lots of pounds to sleep in this bed for a night."

"Is it really that nice?"

She patted the empty spot beside her. He hesitated, but eventually relented.

"Oh, yes. I would spend the pounds as well."

For a moment, they both laid side by side and a part of Irene seriously considered paying for a night at the hotel.

Just then, the door opened. Joe shot sat up, but Irene didn't move.

"Uh, Mrs. Holmes?" Barton stuttered. "The posters ready for you."

"Quite right." She slid off the bed, bidding farewell to the comfortable blankets.

Returning to the other room, she saw a dozen vandalised posters spread out on the dining table just as she'd instructed. Most had a simple, angry red line of paint across Miss Carrington. One had the word "thief" in splotchy letters, and another – the word "murderer". But it was the last poster that caught Irene's attention the most. "Husband Killer" was scrawled in the same red paint.

A very specific accusation.

Irene dug through her bag for her small knife and petri dish, taking a few scrapings of the paint.

"How long have Miss Carrington and Mr. Radcliffe been in London?"

"Only the past three days," Barton supplied.

"And was a big fuss made of them coming overseas?"

"You mean back home? Oh, yes. This is most exciting for us. An international premiere!"

"And obviously you've made it known that they are staying here."

"Miss Holmes, are you implying this is somehow poor planning on my part?"

"I am in no way blaming you. However, Americans have a way of showing off and I'm wondering if that perhaps played a part."

Joe stepped in, hastily sweeping up her clumsy wording. "Meaning no offence, of course. You are simply more... excitable than we are over here."

Irene raised a brow at her friend, but continued on. "Has either actor ever received threats before?"

"None."

"Not even ones you've kept secret from them?"

"No. I tend not to keep much from them as our working relationship has been quite lucrative. Mr. Radcliffe gets the odd letter from an angry husband whose wife has fallen for him now and again, but that never turns into anything. Miss Carrington mostly receives love letters from both men and women."

The man waggled his eyebrows at Eddy, who responded with a polite, if not reserved, smile.

Irene fought the urge to roll her eyes. "Did you mark down where you took each poster from?"

"Yes."

"Excellent." Turning to Eddy, she instructed, "Gather a handful of constables to keep their eyes out for any other posters around the city. If they could gather them, that would be ideal, but if not, then we need their exact location. Please find competent men."

"I will do my best. If you two are fine here, then I shall return to Scotland Yard."

"Of course. I'll ring you later. Goodbye." She focused back on Mr. Barton. "Give the locations of these posters to my colleague. We shall take them with us to analyse further. You may gather them back up now."

As she finished her sentence, the suite door opened. Mr. Barton abandoned all instructions on the spot.

"Ah, Don, come in and meet our guests: Mr. and Mrs. Holmes."

Irene glanced up at their visitor and recognised the man from the posters. Donald Radcliffe, the famous American actor.

His eyes were dark, as was his hair. He was slim, yet had the look of someone who took care of their body and had someone who could tell him how to exercise properly to emphasise his muscles for the silver screen. His face was smooth, his jawline pronounced, with a thin trimmed moustache. By the way he sauntered, she could tell that he was wearing slight lifts in his shoes. A handsome man in any regard, but with too much swagger and pomp for Irene to take seriously.

Don had also been drinking – but not overly so.

While Irene didn't think this man was out vandalising his own film posters at night, he was nevertheless on her suspect list as he had prime access to Miss Carrington.

Don waved away his agent and bee-lined right for her. "Well, hello there, sweetheart," he said, voice smooth and silky, despite the American accent.

"Mr. Radcliffe." Irene held out her hand. "Good to meet you."

The actor gently kissed her knuckles.

Irene yanked her hand away.

"No," she said, then gestured to the couch. "If you would please sit, I'd like to ask you a few questions. This is my partner, Doctor Joe Watson, not Mr. Holmes, as your agent keeps getting wrong."

"Certainly," he drawled with a hair-width less confidence, then turned to Joe. "You know, I played a doctor in a film a few years ago."

Joe grasped his hand. "I was fighting in the war a few years ago."

"Ah, well, thank you for your service."

Her friend's words didn't seem to have any ill effect on Mr. Radcliffe as the actor took up a spot on the couch. Irene sat in the chair across from him, but Joe remained standing directly at her shoulder, in what she recognised as a protective stance.

But what was he protecting her from? The crowd outside was one thing, but here in a room with a singular actor who, though cocky, was certainly no danger. But she said nothing, eager to get on with the interview.

Before Irene could continue her interrogation, Mr. Radcliffe spoke once more. "I don't see a wedding band on your finger."

She crossed her legs, sitting tall. "I don't recall asking if you saw a wedding band."

He flashed a perfect white smile. "You didn't. Just an observation."

Irene gritted her teeth. The man was suave and clearly used to every interaction going his way. She sensed he would attempt to smooth-talk his way out of every question.

What he didn't know, though, was that he was no match for her.

"These posters we've acquired all appear to target just Miss Carrington. Regardless, have you had any threatening letters or any unpleasant encounters?"

He shook his head. "None that I can recall."

"Have you witnessed anything hostile toward Miss Carrington?"

"Nothing except for these posters."

Irene tried to read the actor as best she could, knowing full well that he was used to manipulating himself into any character. But, so far, all she saw was a man who was very aware he was the hottest ticket in town, with a horde of women ready to fawn over him the moment he stepped outside. "Are you concerned at all?"

Don shrugged. "Only if this puts a damper on the premiere."

And there it was. He finally let a weakness slip. Irene watched as he picked at his trousers and swallowed hard.

He was concerned, but not nervous. This could indeed mean innocence in the whole ordeal, but it was still too early to tell.

There'd been no trace of red paint in his bedroom, nor a speck on his expensive suit or fine leather shoes. And quite frankly, Irene couldn't see Donald Radcliffe in a back alley with cheap paint in the middle of the night.

She stood. "This will all be put to bed by the end of the week, I assure you. Is there any other information you can offer or any other worries you have?"

The man stood as well, smirking. "I'm worried I didn't catch your first name."

Ignoring the American's foolhardy attempt at flirting, she turned to Mr. Barton. "Has Miss Carrington arrived yet?"

The agent looked to his client who nodded. "She's in her suite."

"Excellent. We will be brief, so you can get on with your evening."

Mr. Radcliffe stuck out his hand to Joe. "Nice to meet you, Doc. And you as well, Miss Holmes." He shook Irene's hand and gave her a wink.

"My name is Irene," she said, taking her hand from him. "You'd do well to remember it."

"Oh, I certainly will."

She strode out of the suite, with Joe at her heels.

Chapter II
The Curious Locations of Vandalised Posters

As Joe followed Irene to the door across the hallway, he felt his stomach turn a little. Meeting Don Radcliffe was not as he'd expected; in truth, it was slightly underwhelming. The man spent the whole time glued to Irene, which made Joe uneasy – as if his friend was simply a prize that the actor was determined to win.

Miss Carrington would be different. At least, Joe hoped so because he desperately wanted to change his opinions on American actors.

The pair entered the suite where the woman in question stood to greet them.

Irene went forward, hand out, ready to get down to business. "Miss Carrington, pleased to meet you. I am Irene Holmes."

"Lovely to meet you, as well." The actress's voice was deeper than his partner's, and sultry, the sound tickling Joe's ears.

Mr. Barton stepped up next to them. "My god, you look identical."

With the two women in the same room, both in simple make-up, the resemblance was even more striking. The actress's hair was thinner and pulled back, and she wore an expensive dress, whereas Irene was in her trousers and shirt, but they could've passed for sisters at least, or nearly identical twins at best.

Miss Carrington gave a hearty laugh. "I suppose we do. Though I'd give anything to have your abundance of hair. They have to work wonders on mine to get it that thick. Plus, you look like you could take on an army and win."

Irene's lips tugged up. "We *did* take on an army and win."

"You certainly did."

Joe felt a grin form on his own face. Irene had warmed up to Miss Carrington already, which would do wonders for the case. Plus, he was pleased to see his friend receive so many well-deserved compliments.

She gestured to him. "This is my partner, Doctor Joe Watson."

"Charmed to meet you, Miss."

"Well, aren't you handsome. That red hair would do well on film. Your height would cost the studio a bit extra, but you've a face for the screen, for sure."

"Oh, uh." His cheeks warmed, and he knew he was turning scarlet. "Thank you."

"Please sit, Miss Carrington." Irene instructed.

The actress sat gracefully on the sofa, crossing a long leg over the other, keeping a perfect posture. Irene took up the spot across the sofa while Joe sat in the chair beside her.

While her posture could be preposterous at times, Joe noticed that Irene did often sit upright and attentive, especially when on a case. However, he maintained that for this particular interview, she had a straighter back and her toes were pointed gracefully towards the floor while crossing her legs.

Or perhaps that's how she always sat and he simply was overthinking.

Irene wasted no time with her questions. "Have you had any threatening letters or telephone calls? Anyone following you?"

"No," Miss Carrington replied. "I do get the odd letter where someone has expressed their love to me, and I've been shouted at during premieres – usually something about my dress, – but they are promptly dealt with. Now, we've never held a premiere in England before. Perhaps this is someone angry about the fanfare? This city still looks a bit worn down, though it's been a few years since the war ended."

Irene nodded. "We took quite the beating, yes. But we are not inherently mean here in London."

Miss Carrington let out a small gasp, quickly shaking her head. "I didn't mean to offend."

"Oh, you did not."

The actress breathed a wispy sigh of relief. "It's actually my first time here and I am enjoying myself."

"Good. Do you have any thoughts or ideas about who may be vandalising these posters?"

"I'm sorry. I wouldn't have even known about the posters if Kipp hadn't brought them to my attention. And that was only because I pressed the issue. But your police officers have been more than helpful and we've had many who've volunteered to escort us anywhere, or to stand guard outside the hotel. That Detective Lestrade is a proper gentleman; he took this on, even when Don and I thought the whole thing ridiculous."

"Eddy is a good man. He will be glad to help you with anything, or ring us should you need our assistance."

Joe scribbled down as many words as he could in his notebook, but had little to write. Both actors had provided the same information, and neither were too concerned. Even the agent appeared to think this whole affair a nuisance rather than a serious worry.

Perhaps that's all it was: someone still strung out from the war who simply couldn't stand to see rich Americans prancing around London.

Irene hopped to her feet and adjusted her satchel. "We will investigate the venue, as a precaution. Please let us know if anything happens"

Miss Carrington stood as well. "Do you think we are in danger?"

"I am not sure at this point. It's always wise to stay cautious, especially if you are staying in a place where you shouldn't want for anything."

Joe turned to Mr Barton and handed him one of their business cards, of which they were running low. "Keep the staff roster limited. Have them dine in their rooms. And please telephone us if anything looks odd or if you have any concerns."

* * * * *

Irene pulled the Vauxhall in front of the large cinema as Joe glanced up at the darkening clouds. They'd be lucky to get out of the there and back before the rain came down.

"I'm used to the smaller venue just round the corner from Baker Street," he said, marvelling at the building. "But, I suppose for a film premiere, this would be much more suitable."

"Perhaps I should go to the cinema more." Irene glanced at the marquee, displaying "The Thief at Midnight".

"I'm sure you'd love it if given the chance," Joe said, then laughed. "Depending on the film, of course."

They entered the grand foyer where they were met with a large poster promoting the picture. The cinema was empty due to the premiere preparations, and no films were being shown for the next two days.

A man in a suit rushed over to them. "May I help you?"

"I am Irene Holmes and this is my partner, Doctor Watson. We are just here to take a turn about the place and ensure it is safe for the premiere at the end of the week."

The man guffawed. "I can assure you that there shall be no danger. We take security to the utmost importance here. Are you from Scotland Yard?"

He looked them up and down and came to his own conclusion.

Irene answered anyway. "Scotland Yard has hired us to perform this duty. Now, may we look into the theatre? Or, perhaps, even view the film itself?"

"Heavens, no! This is the biggest picture of the year. We cannot simply run the film reel for any couple off the street."

Joe took Irene's arm, feeling the heat rising off her. "Fine, if you will not let us view the film, may we please walk around the venue?"

The guard hesitated; Joe almost begged him to just let them look.

Irene hadn't stepped away, which meant she was using Joe's grasp on her arm to keep calm.

"Sorry, but I would need you to come back with a constable. You talk of safety, and yet here you are, wanting to poke around without so much as an official note."

Joe knew there was no point arguing and almost agreed. While Irene's father might have been known around London, their own little duo had yet to make their way into every nook and cranny. Regrettably, they would have to return with Lestrade or one of his constables. Slight disappointment hung over him as he would've loved to wander around an empty theatre and even get a private screening.

But, right now, his main concern was to extract Irene before she entered the theatre without permission and got them both arrested for trespassing.

He squeezed her arm. "We apologise for taking up your time. We will indeed return with someone from Scotland Yard."

His partner didn't budge at first, but then gave in, spinning on her heels and marching toward the door to the street.

Joe followed her out, and they climbed back into the car. They sat for a moment, like immovable objects. Irene was deep in thought, and stared out the windshield, chewing her lip.

"We will come back. Though it may not be so urgent."

"No?"

She shook her head. "Whomever is defacing these posters is doing it on sight, in the moment. If there has been no attack at The Ritz, then I doubt they would set up some plan at the theatre. Of course, we will still investigate it, but for now, let's dig deeper into the posters."

"I agree," Joe said as she finally started the engine. "Perhaps the posters will solve everything."

"Or they may throw us into an even deeper mystery."

They weren't two blocks from the cinema when Joe spotted a film poster with a bold red line across Miss Carrington's image.

"Stop the car."

Irene pressed the brakes a little too hard, swerving to the side of the road. The vehicle jerked to a halt and Joe hopped out, with the sleuth right behind.

"Oh, Joe," she breathed, hurrying to get ahead of him. "How brilliant of you!"

The poster was stuck to the front of a small bookshop. Having gained a surplus of energy from the discovery, Irene overtook him and arrived first, swiping the red line. It didn't come off on her finger, but the colour smudged on the paper.

"This is fresh. Only a few hours old, if that."

"Done this morning," Joe observed. He looked around the street for any spot a possible witness might be.

A hat shop sat adjacent to them. He nudged Irene, pointing.

"Well done! Collect this poster. I will pop over and see if they know anything."

Irene took off in a fury of honks from passing vehicles.

Joe carefully peeled the poster off the brick. It came off easier than he expected. Rolling it up, he shoved it under his arm and gazed about the street. At the corner was the small but elegant Renaissance Hotel and across from it – an old army supply shop attempting to sell off things people looked to get rid of. Then a cafe and the hat shop Irene stood in.

She returned a moment later with a foul look on her face.

"No luck?"

"People are so dense sometimes. She saw nothing. Streets been busy, though, with the premiere upcoming." She paused and glanced down the pavement. "We'll drive down and around the block, see if we find more posters."

* * * * *

Needless to say, they didn't find any other posters. In the end, they resigned to go back to Baker Street. Inside, the dining table was shoved against the far wall near Irene's bedroom and the couch was pushed forward into the sitting area. All thirteen defaced posters sat on the floor. Irene stood in the middle of the array, slowly turning, inspecting them all.

Several cups of tea were dotted around the room. Joe made a grab for one, hoping it was the most current. Thankfully, the liquid was warm. Meanwhile, outside was pitch black; he knew, without looking at the clock, that it had to be after eleven.

He stood by their large investigations board, a collection of pins in his hand. The most recent one he stabbed in the area with the hat store.

"The only buildings of note in the area where most of the posters were found is a small hotel, a boarding house and the theatre itself. Lestrade's constables have seen no other posters anywhere else in the city?"

"No," Irene confirmed. She'd rung Lestrade when they got back from the theatre, but the DI reported nothing in that short about of time.

"And there's none by The Ritz." Irene poked at one of the posters.

"Well, none that have been spotted. But there are so many fans and constables wandering around the hotel – I highly doubt a vandal would go unnoticed. What do you make of the paint?"

"Cheap. Easy to come by. But the marks get angrier." She rocked back and forth on her heels, staring at the floor, as she spoke.

"Do you think they are in danger?"

She flung her arms up. "I am not sure. This could be something or it could be just a person who does not want the cinema back in London."

Irene stood up and looked around for a way to hop over to Joe without damaging the evidence. He stepped forward and extended his hand, which she readily grasped, launching herself over the posters, landing clumsily next to him.

A slightly selfish thought wiggled its way into Joe's mind as they stared at the map.

"Perhaps we need to make ourselves available all the time. Be by the actors' sides until this premiere is finished."

Irene glanced at him sideways for a brief second before bursting out in laughter. "You mean to have them put us up in a room at The Ritz so we may act as their bodyguards?"

He nodded. Images of the plush carpet, high soft bed and delicious smells from the restaurants swirled around his head.

"Well, I mean…"

He shot his friend a sly smile, but quickly wiped it from his face,

Irene looked at him like a cat about to pounce. "Joe, that may be the most brilliant idea you've ever had."

"Really?" The smile reappeared on his face.

She nodded. "On a purely selfish level, yes, I would leap at the chance to stay there. And we could surely convince them it would be needed."

He thought about the actors' suites. If there was a two-bedroom suite, then they could share the room and still have space for the investigation. They could live like stars and dine with the rich, if only for a few nights.

Joe chuckled at the absurdness of it all. "The only problem with that plan is it would allow Mr. Radcliffe to pursue you more."

Irene rolled her eyes. "He was cheeky, wasn't he?"

"You fired back at him in the most excellent manner, though."

"Thank you."

"One might have almost called it flirting."

She punched him. "Joe Watson, you take that back."

"He was certainly taken by you." He rubbed his arm, laughing.

"*He* was a flirt. I was an investigator."

"You truly were."

Joe let out a cry as he dodged another swing from Irene, dancing backward toward her desk.

She scowled at him, but he caught the playful smirk on her lips.

"It is very late. Go to bed, Doctor. Tomorrow, we will scoop up Eddy and investigate the venue bright and early. Then, *perhaps* we will get ourselves a room at The Ritz."

* * * * *

An hour later, after retrieving Isla from a grumpy Miss Hudson, Joe turned down the comforter on his small single bed; he couldn't help but think of the gorgeous bed at the hotel. Perhaps he should invest in a new mattress and a set of lovely sheets. That would be a nice birthday present for Irene as well.

He climbed into his bed. Though he loved this room, a few nights in a hotel would suit him just fine. He may not even dream as often as he usually did. He never quite remembered all of his dreams, but he knew his mind was active even in deep slumber.

Irene had mentioned once that she had vivid dreams; he wondered how often and if they ever kept her up at night. Did she even remember them or let them flit away like Joe tried to do?

As he laid his head on the pillow, he heard the telephone ring downstairs, its shrill echoing sharp and loud through the flat. He leapt out of the bed and hurried down the stairs, almost slipping in his bare feet, the terrier at his heels.

The telephone rang again. Joe marvelled at how he usually made it all the way downstairs before Irene even emerged from her room.

He scooped up the receiver. "Joe Watson speaking."

In that moment, his partner finally appeared, standing on tiptoes, pressing her ear to the phone.

"It's Lestrade. I'm calling from The Ritz. There's been a murder. It looks brutal. You better get down here quick—"

Irene grabbed the phone from Joe, and the cord wrapped around his wrist.

"Is it either of the actors? Good. We will be there at once."

She set the receiver down, but the cord was still wound around him.

"Both actors are still alive," she supplied as she scampered away to her room. "Get dressed. This escalated quickly!"

Sensing a mystery afoot, Isla barked in excitement. Joe was left standing hunched over, twisting his wrist to free it from the cord.

* * * * *

Half a dozen reporters stood outside the hotel, with twice as many constables holding back bystanders, all trying to see through the front doors. Irene and Joe pushed through them.

Lestrade waved them through the police line and into the building.

"It's a young woman," he said as they strode through the lobby. The three stepped into the lift. Irene shifted a bit closer to Joe as they ascended.

"She came from Mr. Radcliffe's room as she'd spent the evening with him."

"Was she one of Madame Jeannie's girls?" Irene asked.

"I couldn't tell you where she came from, quite honestly. And I don't know Jeannie's girls well enough to say, but I don't believe so. Jeannie keeps her house well-fed and healthy. And this poor lass seems to have missed a meal or two. But, you'd be able to tell me best."

Joe hoped it wasn't one of Jeannie's girls. Not that he knew them particularly well, but they'd been in contact before for cases. He knew Lestrade didn't actively use the Madame's house, but he did visit the woman herself to see about her well-being since they helped Irene during the war.

Irene continued with her questions. "Did Radcliffe come out to investigate the scream?"

Lestrade nodded. "By the time he got out, the woman was bleeding on the ground."

"Did he go near the body?" Irene's voice wavered as the lift jerked to a stop.

"He claims he was halfway down the hall when he saw all the blood. He retreated to his room to ring his agent, who then rang me at my home. The doorman didn't see anyone leave, but an automobile came tearing out of the side street and took off down the wrong side of the road before straitening and driving away."

"Wrong side? Interesting. Did he get the make of the vehicle?"

"Black."

"Wonderful..."

The lift doors opened and the three of them stepped into the hallway. Even there, Joe could catch a whiff of a metallic tinge in the air.

"I will warn you both," Lestrade began. "This is a vicious attack; one of the most violent ones I've seen in a long time."

Two constables stood at one end of the hallway, blocking the body from view. At the other end, Mr. Radcliffe and Miss Carrington stood with Mr. Barton, all looking anywhere but at the crime scene.

Eddy led them toward the actors. "I've cleared them as suspects, but thought you might want a quick chat before they go back to their rooms."

"Quite right," Irene said.

Miss Carrington wore a thick, fluffy robe. She was an apparition clutching a handkerchief in her hand. On the other hand, Mr Radcliffe looked only a little pale and like he'd rather be anywhere else but here. Barton was still in his pyjamas, his face a sickly green.

Irene looked the actress up and down before dismissing her. "You may go back to your room, Miss Carrington. Keep your doors locked and do not travel anywhere without an escort."

Mr. Barton led her back to her room, speaking to her in soothing, if not nervous, tones.

The sleuth then turned to Mr. Radcliffe, who immediately put on a brave face, though Joe caught his clenched fists. She looked him up and down a few times, then spoke:

"You are free to go to your room as well, though I may have some questions once I am finished with my investigation."

She pivoted on her heel and headed toward the crime scene.

With Irene gone, the actor let out a breath. "That scene down there is horrible. How does she so boldly walk up to it?"

Joe gazed down at his friend. "She's seen worse, I'm afraid."

"She's brave."

"Yes, she is. Please, stay safe in your room. If we have any questions, we will find you."

Mr. Radcliffe nodded, but kept his eyes on Irene. The way he looked at her – like he'd drop to his knees and do anything she told him to – sat ill with Joe. He'd seen that look before in many men, most recently from the government agent that pursued Irene a few months ago, and it made him just as uncomfortable now as it did then.

He was protective of his friend, but there was something else that he couldn't quite put his finger on that made him want to defend Irene to the world and also praise her to the very end

He shook it off, angry at himself for feeling petty jealousy, and went to join his friend at the crime scene.

Chapter III

The Mystery Takes a Dark Turn

The body lay face up at the end of the hallway. Dark blood seeped into the plush carpet, pooling around the delicate frame. A fur shawl was thrown a meter away from the victim, while the blue dress she wore was stained with red. Her dark hair splayed out, coagulated and clumped together.

But that wasn't the most noticeable detail about the crime scene. A kitchen knife stuck out of the woman's face, the blade lodged deep into her cheek.

A constable stood near the body, face green. Irene pointed to a collection of doilies on a table at the end of the hallway, clearly placed there by a housekeeper, then forgotten with the excitement of the evening. "Pass me those."

The man hesitated, still trying to avoid staring at the body, but he defeatedly stepped back and grabbed the pile.

Irene snatched the doilies immediately. "You can go. I require space to see what exactly happened."

He eagerly scampered away.

She dropped the pile of cloths close to the body, then hopped onto it, avoiding the blood. No doubt the liquid would seep through, but perhaps it would only get on the bottom of her boots and keep the toes clean. She pulled on a pair of gloves, then tossed her bag behind her, clear of the crime scene.

As Irene studied the body, she heard Joe approach.

"There are more injuries than just the face," she told him. "Get me paper for this knife, Eddy will to examine it later."

Her partner ripped a piece from his notebook, holding it out to her. Grabbing it, Irene crouched and grasped the black, sturdy handle and pulled, causing blood to seep from the wound. It was an army knife that could easily be found in London, as thousands of soldiers flooded into the city during the war.

She motioned to the DI after handing over the murder weapon. "Help me turn her over."

Eddy hopped to the other side, not bothering with his work boots as the blood in the carpet oozed around his feet. He had his own gloves on and together, they rolled the woman face down.

Behind her, Joe gasped. "There's where all that blood is from."

Six slashes adorned the woman's back. They were angled upwards, meaning the attacker was potentially shorter in height.

Irene looked over each slash, then reached forward and ripped the back seam of the dress, revealing bruised skin. While the bruise around the stab wound hadn't fully formed, she knew it wouldn't be bigger than her own fist.

"Once the body is back at the morgue, the bruises on her back will be the size of a woman's fist. This upper one is already showing signs of a small hand."

"You think a woman did this?" Eddy asked.

"Most certainly."

"Shall we interview Miss Carrington again?" Joe chimed in.

"It was not her. She was asleep. There were blanket indents on her arm and her curls on the left side of her hair were slightly flatter than her right. I may have another chat with Mr. Radcliffe, however."

Eddy crouched, pushing a clump of damp hair from the victim's face and kept his voice quiet when he spoke. "Tell me I'm not the only one who sees the resemblance between this victim and Miss Carrington."

Irene frowned at the poor girl. "You are not. And it is certainly not a coincidence."

She looked at her friend. His brow was furrowed and his jaw clenched.

"What is it?" she asked.

He shook his head and straightened. "Nothing.

She held out her hand for Joe as she hopped off the pile of doilies. "The body can be taken away. Though, I would love to see the coroner's report when you receive it."

"You shall. Are you going back to Mr. Radcliffe?"

"I am, but I will interview him alone."

Joe raised a brow. "You think he'd be more inclined to speak about prostitutes with just you?"

"Not necessarily, but his showboating can only go so far before he feels vulnerable, and I crack his shell. With you, he'll get his hackles up like a bulldog, inappropriate jokes may be made, and nothing will actually be accomplished."

"Are you certain?"

"Yes. You can stand outside the door, and I will call if I need you."

Irene gave Mr. Radcliffe's door a sharp knock before letting herself in. Even in the little time between their visit earlier this afternoon and now, the suite had a lived-in feel to it. The cushions were askew, a jacket was draped over the couch and Irene saw a messy bed with the comforters bunched and crumpled through the open bedroom door.

Mr. Radcliffe was dressed in a smoking jacket, pouring a glass of whiskey over ice. Judging by the redness on his neck, this was drink number two.

"Mr. Radcliffe, may I have another few words before I depart?" Irene shut the door behind her.

The man smiled, warmer than she expected. Interviewing him on her own was perhaps the best course of action, after all.

"Anything for you, beautiful." Don held up the whiskey bottle. "Drink?"

Eyeing the dark liquid, Irene *was* tempted to try the expensive alcohol, but ultimately shook her head.

"You don't drink on the job?"

"I don't drink at a crime scene."

He flashed her another grin and sauntered to the couch.

She sat across from him and immediately started into her questions.

"Why did you select that particular girl for your pleasure tonight? Were you given a choice or did your agent select one at random?"

Mr. Radcliffe hesitated, but seemingly more out of surprise at the bluntness of the question. "Kipp knows what I like."

"So, you like girls that look like your co-star and the investigator working on your case? Bold choice."

"That's been my type long before I starred in a picture with Kathleen." He trailed his eyes down Irene's body, the second drink obviously turning him cheeky and frisky.

She crossed her legs and folded her arms, presenting herself as masculine as possible. There was no way this man – whom just spent a night with a beautiful woman who was brutally murdered – would find her brown stained trousers and blocky jacket endearing, especially when she bore her eyes into him as if she could set him on fire from within.

"Walk me through your night. This woman spends the evening with you—"

"A fine and fun evening."

"Indeed. Then she simply… leaves? You pop her out of the room like rubbish on collection day?"

The actor scoffed at her and took a big swig of his drink. "You make me sound like a monster."

"It's one in the morning, making her leaving your hotel room at near midnight. You didn't think to walk her out of the building? Or ensure she got somewhere safe?"

He finished the whiskey and set the glass down on the table with a clang. Irene unfolded her arms and met his defensive demeanour.

"No, I didn't." The American accent made his words sound harsh. "I stayed here and finished my drink. Oh, don't look at me like that. Do you let every man walk you out of some place you've been?"

"That's different. She spent the evening with you."

"Yes, and she was feeling *very* confident in herself."

"And now she's dead."

Mr. Radcliffe finally broke. He leaned forward, elbows on his knees, looking at the ground He let out a long breath. "That attack looked brutal enough that I don't think my being there would've mattered."

She believed him. In fact, him being with his temporary lover may have made it worse, as well as put him in just as much danger.

Irene continued with her questions, but made sure her tone was softer. Her own sympathy surprised her; she chalked it up to all the lessons from Joe on how to be gentle with people in distress. "Do you know where she came from? Which brothel, I mean. Or was she a private escort?"

Don shrugged. "Kipp said she was from a place on Margot Street."

"And Mr. Barton would've picked her up in the same car that he uses to transport Miss Carrington?"

He looked at her with curiosity. "I would assume as much. Why?"

"Just gathering all the facts. Those are all my questions for tonight. Please keep watch over Miss Carrington. I know she has her own people, but an extra eye won't hurt."

The two stood and Mr. Radcliffe gestured to the small bar cart in the corner where the expensive liquor beckoned a taste. His bravado resurfaced. "You sure you won't have that drink?"

"Not tonight."

"Ah, so there is a night in which you would?"

"There are nights where I would do many things, the least of which is have a drink." Irene didn't mean for the words to have any more meaning than what she said. In her mind, she thought about the evenings of chasing murderers and burglars through the streets of London.

Mr. Radcliffe, however, took the comment as something completely different. "Perhaps we will find that night before I travel back to America."

To Irene's shock and horror, her stomach twinged in a nervous and excited way at his cheeky wink. She adjusted the strap on her bag and headed toward the door. That's where she paused, however, remembering the hurt in the actor's eyes when he spoke about being unable to defend the victim.

"Perhaps it was fortunate that you had not been with that young woman tonight. Who knows, maybe we would've ended up with two bodies, which would not do in the least. Good night, Mr. Radcliffe."

He smirked. "Goodnight, Miss Holmes."

Her friends were waiting outside as she shut the door to the suite.

"Did he provide any more insight?" Joe asked.

"Pieces, but nothing to put together yet. Eddy, I have a task for you."

"I'm sure you do."

"Pull the files of murders that happened in the past three days. Stabbings, similar to this one. Look for female victims."

The DI nodded, quickly catching on.

Joe, however, needed clarification.

"What are you thinking, Irene?"

She looked at her friends. "This poor woman was the second victim; the first is either in the morgue or laying in the London streets."

* * * * *

Joe and Irene sat down to breakfast, both only on about five hours of sleep. She yawned before devouring her last egg. Though she'd slept, it had been restless; she'd tossed and turned and had scattered dreams of slash marks and blood soaking into expensive carpets. It was such a violent act, mostly common in a male attacker, but everything about the crime scene told her the culprit was a woman. A very angry or hurt woman.

The door to the flat burst open.

Miss Hudson hurried in, waving a newsprint about. "You both are in the paper!"

Joe grabbed for the issue, stuffing his last bit of toast in his mouth. He looked over the front page, then chuckled.

Irene took the paper from his outstretched hand. The headline read in bold letters:

Violent Attack at The Ritz! Film Stars in Danger!

A large photograph of the hotel's front steps was splashed right in the centre. Constables lined the stairs, and in the very corner, Irene and Joe entered the building. Though their faces were slightly blurred, certain details were unmistakable. Like how she glared at the camera while Joe's big eyes reflected the flash of the lightbulb.

Her friend laughed. "Oh, this is excellent. Miss Hudson, are you able to get extra copies? I would love to send some to my parents."

"Certainly, love. They'll be so proud. You know, Irene, your father was in the papers a few times, by name. And even more where they kept him anonymous. I shall add this to my collection."

Irene stared at the photograph again, studying all the faces of the bystanders. There were only a few women in the picture – those who'd been out late, saw the activity, and hoped to glimpse a star.

"What's the matter?" Joe asked, noticing her furrowed brow. "You are certainly photogenic, Irene. Though you do have a harsh expression."

She ignored him, poring over the photograph again. "None of these are our murderer. All men and too tall. And the few women present are in too much of a fanatic state to be a vengeful killer." She stole a crust from him, then clasped her hands together. "We have a few stops to make while we wait for Eddy to ring us. Go and get dressed."

* * * * *

Their first stop was the army surplus shop down the street from the theatre, where they'd found their own vandalised poster. They questioned the man to see if anyone had purchased an army knife, but he was less than helpful.

"Many people buy many things," he drawled.

Irene burst out of the door after lobbing a swear word at the shopkeeper. She paused on the street, looking up and down.

"We could try other shops?" Joe offered, steering her away. "Or the hotel?"

The front desk of the Renaissance Hotel didn't offer any better information than the army surplus shop. Irene immediately asked if anyone staying here had spoken about the film or if they had travelled to London specifically to view it.

"I simply cannot tell you that." The manager, a pompous skinny man with a nose too large for his face, looked down at her. "If I gave out information on every one of our guests, then what would be the point?"

"This is not The Ritz. I'm sure there are people whose information doesn't matter."

"Come back with Scotland Yard or some other authority and perhaps we'll see."

Irene stared hard at the man. "And perhaps you should wipe the lipstick off your collar before you go home to your wife."

She pivoted on her heels as he stuttered out some answer. She left the hotel in a huff and stood on the pavement, arms folded, tapping her foot in thought. The only thing to do was head back to Baker Street and wait for Eddy's phone call.

* * * * *

The moment Irene and Joe stepped through the door, Miss Hudson came running, an excited Isla at her feet.

"Eddy telephoned not too long ago."

"What did he say?" Irene scooped up the dog so she wouldn't bark over the landlady's words.

"He found the file and that this one is just a grisly, whatever that means, but it doesn't sound pleasant!"

Chapter IV
The Thief at Midnight

Scotland Yard was bustling on this particular morning, alive with chatter about the visiting celebrities and which constables would be on the security line during the premiere.

If there was still to be a premier. Joe worried that, with the way these murders were happening, they'd call of the whole thing altogether.

"They won't cease the premiere," Irene said beside him, as if she could see his thoughts. He looked at his friend in bewilderment. In turn, she pointed to a pair of inspectors in the foyer gossiping about the recent events. "Lord knows nothing could stop the Americans once they make up their minds."

Today was a miserable rainy day in London. Joe kept his raincoat tight to his body, lest he drop water on the stacks of papers on the desks as they passed. A few constables and DIs greeted the pair as they weaved through, aiming for the back offices. Irene, however, confidently strode forward, her long coat billowing out behind her as they reached their target.

Lestrade shared the office space with DI Gregory who wasn't in at this particular moment. Inside were two desks and a few paper cabinets.

The man in question came in behind them, folder in hand. "Good morning to you both. I'm sure you can guess that, with two murders now involved, Scotland Yard has taken over this investigation."

Irene grunted. "It's ours. You gave it to us."

"No, I gave *you* vandalised posters. A double homicide is a completely different circus, indeed. However, I did trade in some favours so I can lead this case, as well as convinced my superiors to let you both stay on."

"That's lovely of you, thanks." Joe jumped in before Irene had a chance to say something snarky.

"How kind, indeed."

Lestrade turned to his childhood friend. "What else would you have me do? You'd end up coming to me anyway, exactly like you did, asking for something or other."

Irene's whole body seemed to react to his words.

Joe grasped her arm.

"We are all tired and this conversation is about to take a dive. So, thank you, Lestrade, for allowing us to help." He looked pointedly at Irene, who rolled her eyes.

But then her gaze fell onto the empty desk beside Lestrade's. "Where's Thom?"

"Away visiting family."

"He'll be quite vexed when he hears that we were dealing with American film stars. Oh, please let me be the one to tell him."

Lestrade raised a brow. "If it pleases you."

"It really would."

The detective shook his head, exasperated, but their tension dispelled. He handed her the folder, but kept his grasp on it as she took it in her hands. "This stays in the office. I've been told that if either of you take another file home, my desk will be back out there with everyone else. Understood?"

Irene nodded, though Joe suspected she hadn't heard a word. She flipped through the file.

"Same cause of death," Lestrade said. "Multiple stab wounds. Angry. And the nose is broken on this one."

As he spoke, she stepped close to Joe, showing him the papers. He sucked in a breath at the sight of a woman, eerily similar to Irene and Miss Carrington, with a bloodied broken nose, pale skin and dead eyes. He felt suddenly thankful that he didn't need the details as Irene would do that work for the both of them. It was true that he'd seen dead bodies before – and fairly gruesome ones at that, but this particular case…

"These make me so uneasy."

"Because they are women?" Irene asked, flipping another page.

"Because they look like you."

Lestrade nodded. "It is unsettling."

They exchanged worried looks. Joe's mind flashed back to her run-in with some men in an alley that had left her bruised to hell and back before Christmas.

His stomach turned.

Irene closed the folder and handed it back to Lestrade, then clasped her hands behind her back and began pacing the room.

"We are missing *why* this woman has a vendetta against Miss Carrington. The actress hasn't even been in London a week! And she surely doesn't socialize as much as I thought these film stars would. It is the 'why' we need to figure out. In the meantime, I don't suppose we could collect all the women in London who look like Miss Carrington, could we?"

Lestrade's eyes widened. "Like, put an ad in the paper? That would get too big. We'd have people from all over the country."

She snapped her fingers. "Quite right. No good. Scratch it from the board."

"I don't have a board—"

"So, what do we do, gentlemen?"

Irene was looking at them both, awaiting their answer. Joe couldn't tell if she didn't know the next step or if she was simply giving them an opportunity to help. Assuming the latter, he looked to Lestrade for assistance. The DI appeared suddenly tired and out of thoughts for the day.

Irene rolled her hand in encouragement but still received no answer. Joe racked his brain for everything that they've attempted to do and what was left to do. Finally, the answer came to him:

"We find out what the picture is about."

Irene grinned at him, her eyes lighting up in glee. "Precisely. Well done, Doctor. Eddy, I expect better next time."

His mouth opened and he threw his hands in the air. "What will watching a picture tell you?"

"Hopefully more than we know now. We will need your assistance, of course."

"To watch a picture? I don't know if that will get approved, especially since—"

"No, Eddy," Irene deadpanned. "We are more than capable of *watching* a picture on our own."

Joe cocked his head, eyes wide. "Irene…"

"Oh, fine. I apologize. We need you to come with us simply to get us into the building as the cinema staff want to see a badge that we do not posses. Though our business card should be enough."

"Well, I can certainly do that. Also, I accept your apology. Please keep me informed though. I don't want you running away with this case because you are doing a part of the investigation without me."

"Deal," she said with a sly smile. "Would you like us to record every line of dialogue as well?"

Lestrade folded his arms across his chest. "Do not test me, Irene, lest I do just that. Now, give me five minutes to talk with my superior, then we will be on our way."

* * * * *

Lestrade followed the Vauxhall to the cinema in his Wolseley. The rain had come on heavy and Irene had to turn on the wiper, the poor flipper doing its best to keep up.

Upon arrival, they met the manager they'd encountered yesterday.

He gave an audible sigh. "As I told you before, I cannot let you view the picture early. I am under strict—"

The DI stuck out his hand, interrupting the man. "DI Lestrade of Scotland Yard. My colleagues must view the picture in question to assist with an investigation involving two murders."

The man recoiled and clutched his chest in a dramatic fashion. "Double murder? Of whom?"

Beside Joe, Irene rolled her eyes and shifted on her feet, clearly eager to get inside.

If Lestrade felt the same anxiety, he didn't show it. He dug his badge from his coat pocket. "We cannot discuss the details, but it is imperative they view the film. If you could prepare that for us, you'd be doing a great service to Scotland Yard, and perhaps be preventing another murder."

"All because of a film?"

"Yes."

The manager hesitated another moment and Joe thought Irene might explode.

He finally relented. "Fine. Follow me."

Before they could walk forward, Lestrade grasped Irene's arm. "Be nice and come to me as soon as you're finished."

"I shall try." She twisted her arm and motioned for the manager to keep walking.

"Don't fret," Joe assured the DI. "We'll let you know our findings." He then bid him farewell and jogged to catch up to Irene.

They stopped at a small coat room just outside the theatre where they were strongly encouraged to leave their wet articles. The man lifted his thick eyebrow as Joe and Irene shrugged off their jackets. Their outfits matched in the oddest way today; Irene sported green trousers and a brown shirt whereas Joe had on brown trousers and a green sweater vest. He made a mental note to initiate a discussion about their outfit choices. Not that it mattered that they often matched, but it did lend itself to odd looks from anyone who noticed.

Finally, the manager led them through a set of large double doors into the dark theatre room. He switched on the lights, the blubs clinking and crinkling to life, and they were welcomed by a large screen and rows of velvet chairs.

"Please choose a seat. I'll have the boys start the projector."

He left the room, mumbling to himself.

Rushing ahead, Irene chose a spot way too close to the screen.

"No." Joe caught her before she entered the row. "A few back."

"Why?" she asked, but didn't move.

He skirted past her to three rows up, scooting right to the middle. "It's rare I get to select my seat in the theatre, as the best ones are usually taken. This one's perfect."

Irene followed and grunted in curiosity. "I did not know there was a science for picking cinema seats."

"In the words of my best mate, there's a science for everything." Joe winked at her.

She set her shoulders, a smile playing on her lips. "Quite right. Now, is this where we are sitting? Or must you do another equation before I plant my bottom?"

He laughed and settled into the seat.

Irene took up the spot beside him and studied the screen. "Hm, this is quite a perfect spot."

Above them, the projector warmed up as the film was loaded into the machine.

"Before the film starts, I must tell you something."

"Oh?"

She rarely, if ever, gave warnings. Normally, she started right into her narration and expected everyone to drop what they were doing to listen. Joe couldn't fathom what this was about, though, as they'd been side by side for the past 48 hours with this case. Unless it was something so meaningless and he was overthinking it, as usual. Perhaps Irene was just exercising some social graces.

He almost snorted out loud. She'd rarely oblige out in public, let alone when it was just the two of them.

Irene took a breath. "I do not want you to worry about me."

Concern seeped into him and he shifted in his seat. "I don't understand."

A thousand scenarios rushed through Joe's head in an attempt to figure out what she was talking about. Was she going away? Was she suffering from some illness? No, surely she would've told him if this was something serious. Hell, she complained to him almost every month about her menstrual cramps if they were bad enough.

Before he could form a question, though, she continued. "I noticed your reaction to the murdered woman back in Eddy's office. Then you looked at me as if you wanted to put me in a jar to keep me safe."

Joe sighed, relieved that it was nothing that impacted her well-being. Of course she'd seen his reaction back at Scotland Yard; Irene saw everything. She wasn't wrong, either, because that's precisely how he'd felt in that moment. A part of him still felt that way.

"I'm allowed to worry about you, Irene. You're my best mate."

She shot him a sharp glare, but he knew it was a front, an act she put on because she had trouble dealing with people's love toward her.

"I know," she finally spoke. "But do not look at me as if I am so delicate you want to keep me on a shelf so I don't break."

"Some days, that's exactly what I want to do." He laughed as her expression soured even more. He wrapped his arm awkwardly around her shoulders, pulling her as close as the theatre seats allowed. "But I won't, I promise. You'd probably just jump off the shelf and injure yourself, anyway."

Irene rested her head on his shoulder for a moment before the whir of the projector broke them up. However, Joe was in no rush to let her go. Despite her telling him not to worry, the images of her two murdered doppelgängers made him want to hold on to her even tighter.

But, in true Irene fashion, she sat straight and leaned forward, ready to study the film as if it were a lecture from the university.

* * * * *

For the next two hours, Joe was enthralled with "The Thief at Midnight". Miss Carrington's character, a feisty woman named Jane, was determined to steal from one of the city's wealthiest men. Meanwhile, Mr. Radcliffe played a devilish rogue and rival thief after the same treasure.

At one point, Jane poisoned a villain out to capture her, making the death appear like a heart attack. The dead man's wife went after her, but Jane made a daring escape out a window. True to Hollywood fashion, Miss Carrington and Mr. Radcliffe's characters fell madly in love and ended up working together before driving off into the sunset with their stolen loot.

Joe glanced at Irene a few times throughout the film. She never moved from her hunched position, fingers clasped and pressed to her lips. He had no idea if she was enjoying the film or picking it apart, or both.

The picture ended and Irene sat back, eyebrows still furrowed.

Grinning, Joe turned to his friend. "Well, that was grand. What did you think?"

"Would you like my opinion on the case or the film?"

"The film, then the case."

"There were several inaccuracies regarding the heist jobs. First, the outfits were wildly unfit and too bright. And they moved much too fast. Once during a burglary, I waited an entire hour for a man to move before I stole a small bust for my father. Also—"

"Okay, I get it," Joe chuckled. "You didn't enjoy it."

"You're mistaken. I thoroughly enjoyed it. The action was very well done and the chemistry between Miss Carrington and Mr. Radcliffe was quite palpable."

"Well, that's good then!"

"It is. I'll have to join you at the cinema more often."

He clasped his hands together, excitement jolting through him. He'd asked her countless times, but Irene had always turned him down. So, he'd eventually given up. But this new revelation thrilled Joe to no end. There were so many films he wanted to show her. Sure, she would pick them all apart, but if she enjoyed this one, then maybe she'd like others – perhaps "The Wizard of Oz" and its incredible transition from black and white to colour. Or "Gone With The Wind" and how she just might see a bit of herself in the feisty Scarlett O'Hara. Oh, how he wished he could bring all those films back to the cinema. His mind threatened to run away with the thought until Irene snapped her fingers.

"Murders, Joe. Come back from wherever you went."

"Yes." His cheeks warmed. "What did you glean from the film?"

She pulled her legs up into the plush chair. "What did *you* glean?"

"Uh," he stuttered. "Both leads fell in love… but that doesn't apply to real life as they are simply colleagues. Miss Carrington's character murdered someone—"

"Precisely!"

"Miss Carrington is trying to murder someone?"

Irene shook her head. "No. She is innocent. I think our murderer is operating under a delusion. Come. We've much to do."

She slipped out of the row and down the pathway to the door. Joe quickly followed her out into the lobby.

"Our jackets, Irene!"

The manager was waiting for them, a grin on his face. "Won't the audience simply love the picture!"

Irene waved him off. "Yes. Fine film. Where is your telephone?"

"Right behind the counter. Is everything—"

She brushed past him.

Joe mumbled an apology and followed.

"I have a task for Eddy." She leapt behind the counter to grab the device. "Retrieve our coats, then it's back to the hotel!"

Chapter V

A Proposition from an American Actor

In truth, they stopped home to freshen up before they headed to The Ritz and met with the actors. Irene had given Eddy specific instructions to follow that would take him some time to accomplish.

By late afternoon, they pulled up behind Eddy's Wolseley at the curb of the hotel. Thankfully, the rain had let up dramatically, but that meant an even larger crowd had gathered out front, with double the constables.

When Irene exited the car, a few reporters turned her way. She folded her arms and glared. "If any of you take even so much as one photo of me, I shall ruin your careers overnight."

They all hesitated, but one young, bold boy started to raise his camera. Joe grabbed a hold of her arm and tugged her sideways. "There must be a back door. C'mon."

Sure enough, a side door guarded by a constable sat in the small alleyway. They slipped in and headed up the stairs to a second-floor meeting room. While chatting in a suite was lovely, Irene needed everyone to focus on her plan, which wasn't possible while lounging on comfortable sofas.

The room, which was named after a prince or other famous person of no consequence to Irene, was a smaller space. In the middle was a large table surrounded by chairs, with walls adorned with paintings of what appeared to be the Scottish countryside.

Mr. Radcliffe, Miss Carrington, Eddy, and Mr. Barton were already inside. Joe settled in beside the DI, but Irene remained standing.

"Doctor Watson and I watched your film." She addressed to the two actors. "I have qualms with it, of course, but it is hard to get realism correct in Hollywood. Otherwise, it was very well done."

Mr. Radcliffe huffed a laugh as he lit a cigarette. "A review for the papers, to be sure."

She ignored him, continuing with her narrative. "What we are dealing with is an American woman who has followed you both over here to exact revenge on Miss Carrington. She is under the impression that you have killed her husband in the same manner as your character."

Mr. Radcliffe froze, the cigarette hanging on his lips. Eddy and Joe raised their eyebrows, and poor Miss Carrington sunk in her seat.

"I haven't… I wouldn't…"

"Of course not. But when someone is living a delusion, it is hard to pry them out of it. There is no mistaking that she is after you, as seen by the similar appearance of the murder victims. Both were violently attacked and—"

"Both?" The two actors chimed in together.

"Yes. We found a girl murdered a few days ago in the same manner. And both victims faces were angrily injured. The first had a broken nose and the latest, as you know, took a knife to the cheek. These outbursts occurred when our murderer saw the women up close and realised they were not Miss Carrington."

The actors exchanged worried looks. Meanwhile, their agent leaned forward, eyes practically rolling in their sockets.

"I don't even know where to begin," he started. "How do you know she's American?"

Irene attempted to suppress a grin – she'd learned that smiling during a murder investigation was frowned upon – but she relished lecturing the lesser-minded.

"The automobile driving from the hotel crime scene hurried down the wrong side of the road. In the police report from the first murder, it was noted that the same vehicle was seen weaving on the wrong side – or rather the American side – when fleeing. I asked DI Lestrade earlier today to do some investigations. Tell us, Eddy, what you discovered?"

Eddy straightened and cleared his throat before speaking. "I looked into any American staying around the theatre, where the majority of these posters were found and where our first victim worked out of. While there were many visitors, only seven fit your criteria: arriving within days of Miss Carrington and young enough to perform such brutal acts."

Irene was about to congratulate her friend, but Mr. Barton spoke quick and worried. "So, what are we to do? Arrest all of these Americans?"

"No," she snorted. "That would be silly. I believe the woman we seek will be at the premiere. She will use a cover, just like in the film. A cleaner, perhaps, or some other person milling about. There will be a lot of people at the premiere, giving her ample opportunity to sneak around unnoticed. I think she will attack Miss Carrington there."

Barton shook his head. "But it's so public."

Irene shrugged. "At this point, I don't believe she cares. She is out for blood and may act in the middle of a crowd. However, we can prevent this by forcing her to follow her target to a secluded area before she attacks. Then we can arrest her and prevent any collateral damage."

"And you're certain she'll attack at the premiere?"

"Yes. It's almost a guarantee that the person who shows up at the premiere of "The Thief at Midnight" will be Miss Carrington herself."

The agent stared at her. "Miss Carrington *will* be at her premiere."

"Of course she will. But perhaps not quite."

Irene looked at the actress, who'd been still as a statue for the entire conversation. She was quick to catch on.

"Oh my god," she said softly, big worried eyes fixing on Irene. "*You* are going to be *me*."

Irene beamed and everyone else in the room stirred.

Barton looked her up and down, scoffing. "*You* are going to walk the carpet next to Don? *You* are going to greet the press? Surely you are joking, Miss Holmes."

"I do not joke when there are murders happening." Irene stared him down. "It is a good plan, but I will admit that while we appear very similar, we do have our differences up close.

Therefore, I will need to consult an expert on whether it is even possible. We will meet at Miss Carrington's suite tomorrow morning at nine o'clock sharp to begin our preparation."

"Miss Carrington has her own makeup artist. He's arriving tomorrow and can do whatever's needed"

"No one will be touching me except my own makeup artist. Now, it is almost dinner. Doctor Watson, DI Lestrade, and I will be stopping by the dining room to eat a fine meal on your tab. We shall see you all tomorrow morning. Good evening."

Irene exited the room without waiting for the men to catch up; her mind had shifted to a medium-rare steak and potatoes.

* * * * *

The three of them had the most delicious steak any of them had ever eaten, After dinner, they made their way home full and sleepy.

That night, Irene lay awake, staring into her dark bedroom. She truly hoped that she could look enough like Miss Carrington to make it into the building. She was nervous about the whole affair and it stirred anger in her. Working undercover was a breeze; her father had taught her from such an early age how to fool people.

But this time felt different.

She was playing another person, a very well-known individual who'd been in the spotlight for years.

She yawned and attempted to sway her mind from such anxious thoughts. Instead, she pictured all the ways she would rob a wealthy man better than the film portrayed.

* * * * *

On their way to The Ritz the next morning, Joe appeared particularly worried. He fidgeted in the passenger seat, his leg bouncing up and down.

Finally, Irene sighed. "Speak, Joe. It's as if we just met and you are nervous to tell me something."

"It's because sometimes I don't fancy your wrath. Besides, whatever I say won't matter in this particular instance."

"Speak it, anyway."

"This plan of yours, to go undercover, is dangerous. Are you sure it is the right call?"

"What else would you have us do in so little time?"

"I'm not sure, honestly."

"This plan will work. You will act as my bodyguard, and Eddy will be on the sidelines. I am not in any danger."

"Oh, my worry for your safety is low compared to my worry of you pretending to be someone else."

Irene laughed. "I felt the same last night. But I shall practise all Miss Carrington's mannerisms and simply move quickly through the doors and into the theatre. It will work, my dear Joe." She paused for a moment before saying, "Of course, this is all dependent on if I can even be made up to look like Miss Carrington."

"And if you can't?"

"Then perhaps we simply arrest all American women in London."

This suggestion made Joe smile, which eased her own anxieties.

* * * * *

Irene and Miss Carrington sat next to each other on a sofa in the actress's suite, backs straight, staring ahead. Madame Jeannie's tall frame moved between them, occasionally bending to study their faces.

She was the only person Irene trusted – and wanted – to touch her; she knew that the Madame was an expert in all things beauty.

Also, though Jeannie was a woman of the world, the chance to bring her into the depth of The Ritz and watch her face light up was something that Irene surprisingly relished. The fact that something so seemingly trivial made her friend so happy made her feel good.

Now, a small part of her regretted this whole thing as Jeannie poked and prodded her. Miss Carrington was obviously used to this sort of nonsense – she turned her head every which way with little direction, knowing exactly what Jeannie wanted.

Irene, however, struggled.

Finally, the Madame stepped back.

"It can certainly be done," she said, tucking in a stray dark curl that had fallen from her up-do. "Though we'll have to do some work on Irene's eyebrows since you Americans like them thin. But, with some makeup, and a lesson in mannerisms, you should be able to pass no problem."

Mr. Barton, who'd been hovering in the corner in complete awe of Jeannie, stepped forward. "They sound nothing alike."

"I'm not a fool, I can hear that. Unfortunately, as much as she tries, our dear Irene could never make her voice that low and sultry. So, we will start a rumour that Miss Carrington is feeling a bit under the weather. You can tell everyone she doesn't want to get too close, lest she get them ill as well. That should keep most people away and give her an excuse to keep her mouth shut. But, Irene, I must stress this: keep your composure. I'm sure Miss Carrington will tell you horror stories of all the things people have said to her."

Irene set her shoulders. "I can stay calm."

Jeannie patted her head fondly. "You have proven that you can, but only by the hair on your chin."

A knock came from the door. Irene invited the newcomers in, wanting to end the conversation.

Joe and Mr. Radcliffe entered the suite.

"Jeannie," Joe beamed. "Wonderful to see you!"

"Oh, Doctor!" She glided forward and wrapped him in a hug, almost towering over him in her heels. "It's always a pleasure."

Mr. Radcliffe let out a low whistle and sidled up to the Madame. "If I'd have known you'd be in here, sweetheart, I would've come knocking sooner. You are tall and glorious."

Jeannie turned to Irene. "See what I mean about inappropriate comments? The temptation to smack him is overwhelming, but I remain stoic and calm and I giggle. Tee-hee."

"I can smack him for you."

This earned her a wide-eyed look from Joe and a giggle from Miss Carrington.

And yet the cheeky actor was not phased by the threat, his eyes sparkling. "Are you a makeup artist? Stylist? We've lots of jobs on the film sets."

Jeannie fixed her eyes on him but gestured to Irene. "My darling, be so kind as to tell this gentleman what I do for a living."

"She runs a brothel for lonely men such as yourself who need a confidence boost."

"Oh dear. I should not have given you free rein like that," Jeannie laughed. "But yes, that is what I do."

It didn't deter Mr. Radcliffe, though. "A house of women, eh? Perhaps I should stop by for a visit."

From the corner of her eye, Irene saw Joe debate whether or not to step in. His cheeks were red, though, and she couldn't help but smile.

Madame Jeannie was perfectly capable of handling herself.

Miss Carrington watched with fascination, a look of awe on her face.

"Oh, love," Jeannie said to Mr. Radcliffe. "My girls would chew you up and spit you out."

"Sounds like something I may enjoy."

"In your dreams, handsome." She patted his cheek, then turned to Irene. "I will be back tomorrow to fix you up. I'm sure Miss Carrington has a suitable dress."

"I have more than enough."

"Wonderful. See you then."

The Madame breezed by Mr. Radcliffe without so much as a look back at him. The actor watched her leave, then wandered over to the bar cart to pour himself a drink.

Miss Carrington stepped up beside Irene. "I like her. She's the kind of character you'd love to see in a film, but nobody would be so bold. So, Miss Holmes, what's next?"

"We order some food, as I am famished. Then I learn how to be you for the rest of the afternoon." She turned to the men. "Unless you would also like to learn how to act like Miss Carrington, then we are finished with you boys."

Mr. Radcliffe clapped his hand on Joe's shoulder. "Perhaps we will order our own food and discuss how Doctor Watson here will behave during the premiere."

Joe looked at Irene as they were leaving. "We'll be right across the hall if you need us. See you in a few hours."

Once they were gone, Irene immediately went to work. She lined all the standing mirrors from the suite in the sitting area with Miss Carrington.

"Just like a ballet class," Miss Carrington said.

"Precisely. Now walk and I shall follow."

* * * * *

For the next few hours, Irene mirrored and mimicked Miss Carrington. She perfected the actress's walk, how she nodded, and even how she bent her wrist in a feminine manner when she laughed. As they ate their lunch, the actress explained how premieres went and what was expected. Even though they'd start the rumour that the actress was ill, Irene would still be obliged to curtsey and shake hands.

By dinner time, both women were exhausted. Irene bid good night to Miss Carrington and stopped by the restaurant on her way out. She took home two plates on the film studios tab and headed to Baker Street.

She came home to a quickly written note from Joe stating that he'd taken Sarah out for dinner. The way he scribbled, his letters tired and annoyed, told Irene that perhaps he'd forgotten a planned date again.

Irene ended up giving the second plate of food to Miss Hudson, who raved about the meat and potatoes, and attempted to figure out what herbs they'd infused into the roast beef.

Later, she was halfway through her scribblings from the day of lessons, when the telephone rang.

"Irene Holmes speaking."

"Miss Holmes, how are you? It's Don Radcliffe."

She was instantly on alert. "Has something happened?"

"No. Not at all."

His words were calm and confident, which made Irene even more suspicious.

"Then what's the nature of this call? Did you remember a piece of information?"

She heard him chuckle. "No, Miss Holmes. Irene, if I may?"

"You may."

"I want to take you out. Or have you come over here. I like you; I think you're the most fascinating woman I've ever met. I'd love to get to know you more before I go back home."

At first, Irene was too stunned to speak. Was this man seriously asking her on a date? Sure, he'd been flirtatious with her, but she hadn't reciprocated at all. At least, she didn't think she had. Or was she simply a challenge for him?

"I will not entertain a date while working on a case."

"Then it's not a date. It's two people making pleasant conversation."

She spun and leaned against the wall, phone pressed to her ear. "You are still a suspect, Mr. Radcliffe."

"How about when you clear my name?"

Irene laughed despite herself. "I will entertain the idea of a few hours with you, *if* your name is clear when this is all done."

Behind her, two sets of footsteps entered the flat. She nodded a greeting to Joe and Sarah as they made their way to the couch.

"I'll take that deal, then. Sure I can't persuade you sooner?"

She twirled the phone cord in her fingers. "If you push me too much, I might think you are a legitimate suspect."

Don laughed; the sound was light and pleasant, but telling that he'd had a drink or two. "Then I shall wait until you've caught the bastard doing this. Have a wonderful evening, beautiful."

Her cheeks warmed at the compliment. "You as well."

"What? No handsome?"

"You have to earn a compliment from me, Mr. Radcliffe."

"Oh, ho, but I do love that. I'll do my best."

She hung up the telephone and attempted a scowl, but ended up just glaring. She turned to properly greet Joe and Sarah, but found her friend directly behind her, with a big grin on his face.

"Were you just *flirting*?"

She pushed past him, aiming for her chair by the fireplace. "Of course not."

But Joe didn't let up, following her to the sitting area. "Your cheeks are red. What did he say to you?"

Sarah turned to her, intrigued. "Who was that?"

Irene hesitated, but decided the two of them would only press her for more answers. Besides, it did not matter if they knew the actor was flirting with her. He flirted with everyone under the sun.

Except he'd sought her out.

In an effort to keep her cheeks from reddening any further, she waved her hand. "Don Radcliffe."

Sarah gasped. "Oh goodness. The actor? Joe said you were working with them, but I had no idea he had your telephone number."

Irene attempted to turn the conversation to anyone but herself. "I've only had a handful of conversations with him, but Joe spent all afternoon with him today."

Sarah shifted on the sofa to look to her boyfriend. "Marnie is *in love* with him. Oh, she will be so jealous."

Irene snorted and tossed a log on the fire. "His ego is as big as America itself, but even I will admit that there is a certain dashing quality about him."

Joe guffawed as he sat next to Sarah. "I think that's the first time I've heard you speak about a man like that."

Irene turned, hands on her hips. "I pay you compliments all the time."

"You've never called me *dashing*."

"I think you're dashing." Sarah squeezed his arm.

Joe looked at her as if suddenly remembering she was in the room. Irene noticed the small way he shifted toward her, attempting to include the girl in their banter.

"You should see the suit he has for the premiere, Sarah. It cost more than all my clothes put together."

"And you get to wear a borrowed one that is just as expensive," Irene reminded him. She'd never seen him in a suit and, for some reason, pictured him in a bow tie rather than a classic one.

Sarah's eyebrows pulled together. "You never told me you're going to the premiere."

Irene nodded. "Yes, should be quite the show. We're there to make sure nothing goes wrong."

The young woman looked between them both, then fixed her gaze on Joe. "Oh, but you do live an exciting life, don't you?"

Irene stared at her, trying to figure out her body language – there was frustration brewing, aimed toward Joe, but she couldn't figure out why.

He patted her arm. "I'll take you to the cinema as soon as the film has premiered."

"That'll be three times you would've seen it, then."

As soon as Irene spoke, she felt the air thicken. The couple both stiffened. Sarah wouldn't drag her eyes away from Joe, shoulders tense. He, in turn, looked like a rabbit caught in a trap.

"Three times?"

He hesitated.

When he finally spoke, his word were apologetic. "Well, once at the premiere, once with you, and… Irene and I caught a private screening yesterday."

"Just you two?"

"Yes, sorry. I thought I mentioned that."

Irene felt the need to assure Sarah that this was all part of the case and nothing more. However, some emotion that she didn't understand still sparked between the three of them. All she knew was that, while Sarah liked Irene, she had reservations about her living arrangement with her boyfriend, especially since she and Joe had been together for almost a year and not yet engaged.

As much as Irene wanted to plant herself and watch this unfold from an anthropological viewpoint, she knew the right thing to do was excuse herself.

"I am off to bed. Sarah, I will attempt to get Don's autograph for Marnie if I get the chance."

She hurried into her bedroom and shut the door behind her, fighting the temptation to put her ear to the door and listen.

Chapter VI

Another Glass of Champagne for Doctor Watson

Joe knew he'd messed up, but wasn't quite sure how. Sarah sat silently beside him on the sofa. He didn't know what she was thinking or what to do next. His nerves got the better of him and he attempted to smooth over the situation.

"Do you want to stay for a cup of tea? Once Irene is in bed, she doesn't come out of her room. We could also go to my room. I mean, you haven't even seen it. I am thinking of getting new sheets, or a new mattress."

He remembered his and Irene's conversation about sheets and mattresses on the bed at The Ritz. His ears grew hot, guilt engulfing his stomach. He shouldn't be thinking about his friend when his girlfriend was upset.

Sarah stood abruptly and grabbed her purse. "Actually, I think I'll go home."

She headed into the hallway and Joe dashed to catch up to her. He stopped her at the top of the stairs.

"Wait, please. I don't understand."

Sarah sucked in a breath and looked at him, her blue eyes rimmed with tears. "I'm not your top priority, am I? I mean, us. This relationship."

"What? Of course you are."

"Not when you're on a case."

"There's been murders in this one."

Sarah kept her voice low, but her words were angry. "A few weeks ago, you disappeared into the countryside and stayed in a hotel for two nights with Irene, while I had no idea."

"I… I told you when I got back…" He also hadn't told her that a bullet had grazed his side as it wouldn't have done anyone any good. She would only be insistent that he take a break from solving mysteries. Joe should've stopped talking, but the panic propelled his words. "Irene and I are friends. I've told you—"

"Irene isn't my main worry. I know that she doesn't understand the social cues or limits of your friendship, regardless of how much you've tried to explain it to her. Up until I heard her flirting just now, I thought she was incapable of any romantic feelings at all."

More guilt settled in his stomach like a hard lump of dough. He hadn't been trying hard at all to curtail Irene's overstepping in regards to their friendship. There weren't too many boundaries he enforced; he let her touch and hug him as much as she pleased. And he did the same, though not in quite the boisterous sense.

His touch made his friend happy, her arm in his kept her on course and his hand around her wrist kept her calm. And in return, her fingers in his had helped him quell his episodes.

And sure, they went off together, but that was their job. Lots of their investigations required late nights in clandestine locations.

Perhaps, that was Sarah's point?

Confusion swirled around the guilt in his gut. Joe hoped that if he played dumb, she would keep talking and he could figure it out.

Thankfully, she did so, fiddling with her purse strap. "I know you love investigating crimes, but I thought your heart was with the veterinary practice? It's certainly secure and has a steady income. More so than crime-solving. I know you both have been paid handsomely for some of the cases, but there is no security. There is simply the whim of whatever Irene decides to investigate, whether or not there's payment at the end. We need security for our future, Joe."

He nodded, his body on the verge of a panic attack. "I know. I am considering our future. But I…"

He trailed off and involuntarily looked at the door to the flat.

The panic attack was right around the corner and he was desperate to stave it off. He hadn't had one in so long and he hated that a simple conversation was enough to trigger one.

Sarah took his hands. "You are not responsible for Irene's future."

"I am," he said, the need to defend his friend, pushing through the panic. He tried to backtrack and save this conversation. "I just mean, it's complicated."

Sarah dropped his hands. "Well, uncomplicate it. Finish this case, then we'll have to decide what *our* future looks like. Because I'm ready to move forward with you."

"Our future" rang out in his head, but no matter how much he tried, all Joe pictured was 221b, a roaring fire, cups of tea, Isla at his feet and Irene in her chair. He tried to drag his mind to what Sarah considered their future to be and his stomach flipped. She wanted a house in the country, loads of children and a veterinarian husband.

And until this moment, he'd thought he wanted that too.

But now he had no idea. His head was too full of murder victims that looked like Irene to think straight.

After a few moments, he nodded, feeling the anxiety settle back in.

Sarah kissed his cheek before heading out into the evening.

Joe blew out a breath, but it did little to ease the panic. He did need to sort all his feelings out, because this wasn't fair at all.

But the middle of a case was not the time to do it.

At least that's what he told himself.

He stepped back into the flat, his mind swirling with conflicting thoughts.

Irene froze outside her bedroom, eyes wide, hand on the door, looking as suspicious as Isla whenever she stole a sock.

He startled and clutched his chest. "What are you doing?"

"I was not eavesdropping, I promise. Well, I stepped out to go to the lavatory and heard mumbles and I tried to listen, but I couldn't make out what was being said."

She had been caught – something which rarely happened, and Joe found it hilarious. His conversation with Sarah dissipated and he pushed it right out along with the panic, which melted as soon as he saw Irene.

Two curlers drooped out of a lopsided hair-do. Her pyjamas were mismatched – the bottom of which belonged to him – and she wore his right slipper and Miss Hudson's left.

"Are you alright?" She asked, a third roller threatening to fall.

"Yes," he said, desperate not to think of the implications of his girlfriend winding him up and Irene easing his stress. "I am now."

"Can I know what you both were talking about?"

"Not tonight. I'm not sure I even understood it."

It was a lie, but one hopefully good enough.

Irene saw right through his facade, but accepted his answer nonetheless. "Okay. Get some sleep. We've a big day tomorrow. Goodnight, my dear Joe."

She twirled away from him and entered her bedroom. A curler finally popped off her head and fell to her floor just before she shut the door.

Joe rubbed his head as tiredness blanketed him. He needed to be on point tomorrow, which meant a full night sleep was needed.

* * * * *

He woke late the next morning and had almost the whole day to himself as Irene headed to the hotel to begin her makeover. Sipping his third cup of tea, he couldn't get the conversation with Sarah out his mind; it plagued him as he crunched on a biscuit.

Though Irene had calmed him immeasurably by simply being herself, Joe was frustrated that he had to take time away from the case to sort his thoughts. It also distracted him from the dangerous task she was embarking upon.

The flat was empty of its usual hustle. Miss Hudson had gone ahead to assist where she could. The older woman had been beside herself when Irene asked and put on her nicest daytime dress, complete with matching fascinator.

When it was time, Joe took Isla on a small walk before giving her a bone and bidding her farewell. Then, he climbed into a taxi for The Ritz. Upon arrival, he snuck in through the back door and headed up to the suites.

Mr. Radcliffe answered the door quickly when Joe knocked. "Ah, Doctor. Come in. Just in time for late lunch!"

The actor beckoned him in to a feast of sandwiches and vegetables. There was a bottle of champagne, which Radcliffe poured into flutes. The two clinked glasses. Joe had never had champagne before, but he enjoyed it much better than wine. The first glass went down too easily and Radcliffe quickly poured them another.

As they ate and drank and killed time, they chatted about the weather and what else there was to do in London besides attending film premieres. At one point, Mr. Barton came in and explained Joe's job for the evening. He practised how close he should walk to Irene, as well as how to proceed if someone were to get too close. The instructions weren't much different from what he already did. Most of that was simply gentlemanly manners, but the other reason was because he feared for the public's safety should they get too close to his friend.

As the time approached to pop across the hall and see how Irene's transformation was coming along, Radcliffe poured them yet another glass of champagne. A light buzz had started around Joe's head, however, so he held the champagne for now, planning to sip it slowly.

Radcliffe, too, hesitated before indulging in his fourth drink of the day. He furrowed his brow and spoke in the most serious tone that Joe had heard come from him yet. "I hope I'm not stepping on anyone's toes, Doctor."

"In regards to what?"

"You and Miss Holmes. I didn't want to pursue her without checking if you two were together."

Joe held back a chuckle and was tempted to warn Radcliffe off altogether. Irene hadn't even looked at the man twice, let alone agreed to have him pursue her.

"I'm already with someone else," he said instead, taking a small sip.

"Good. As much as I love women, I don't want to take another man's. I didn't think you were together, but thought I'd check before I took her out. I just have to get her to say yes. She's already a maybe," Don winked. "Now, should we head across the hall to our twins?"

Joe nearly choked, head now full of questions. Had that been what he called to ask Irene last night? She'd told him *maybe*? That panic started in the pit of his stomach again but he drowned it with the rest of his drink. He grabbed another on his way out the door, following Radcliffe across the hall.

There was no reason to panic or feel the way he did. Irene was an adult and could make her own decisions, especially regarding her love life. But Joe was protective; he knew this man was a womaniser and would leave to go back to America soon. There was no future in a relationship with him. But, the way he spoke, it was clear he didn't want a relationship with Irene – only a night or two.

That thought made his stomach flip and the alcohol bubbled up again. His ears burned as he tried to think of anything other than his friend and an intimate night in the same vein.

Luckily, Miss Hudson appeared at the door and stole his attention.

Inside, Miss Carrington sat on the sofa chatting with Lestrade, as the landlady paced in front of the large bedroom door.

"They are just getting her dressed. It's amazing what that Miss Jeannie can do."

Right on cue, the door opened and Madame Jeannie waltzed out, with Irene in tow. Joe almost dropped his glass.

Irene was adorned in a silver sparkled floor-length gown with slim straps and fabric that was nipped and tucked perfectly to the curves of her body. Her hair was puffed and curled in a modern style she'd never tried, pushed back on one side, the other long and in soft waves. Her eyebrows were thin and her makeup gave her eyes a smokey look. Her usual victory red lips were replaced by a slightly darker shade.

Irene looked both gorgeous and not like herself at all.

Radcliffe let out a low whistle and walked up to her. He extended his hand with a grin. She laid her fingers in his and dipped herself in a delicate curtsey with a smile that wasn't her own at all. The actor planted a kiss on her knuckles and, though she cringed, she didn't yank her hand away.

Jeannie shooed him and circled Irene, admiring her work. "Once we did the hair and the eyebrows, it didn't take much makeup."

All Joe could do was stare. The champagne buzz grew louder in his ears. There was no doubt Irene was stunning, but there was something else he couldn't quite put his finger on. Perhaps it was the way Mr. Radcliffe so boldly walked up to her and kissed her hand or that she was about to appear in front of hundreds of people and he couldn't protect her like he wanted to should something go wrong.

Lestrade stood from the sofa. "I'm going ahead to ensure my men have the venue secured. Miss Jeannie, fine work, as always." He paused at Joe and eyed the glass of champagne. "Keep an eye on our girl out there."

"I always do."

"I know." Lestrade clapped him on the shoulder before heading out.

"I'll walk you out," Radcliffe said. "In my excitement to see Miss Holmes, I've forgotten my jacket."

Both of them left, chatting away about some film Lestrade had viewed last week.

Jeannie had noticed a flaw on Irene and scowled. "Oh, Irene, come back here. Over to the window. Let's catch the evening light before it goes away."

Miss Carrington stood and wandered over to help as well.

Joe stayed on the opposite side of the room, sipping. Even though he was dressed in such an expensive suit, he still felt like he couldn't measure up to his friend's beauty. While he may not be the one walking through the premiere with her, he was determined to look his best.

He fiddled with his bow-tie as Miss Hudson came up to him. "She does look stunning, doesn't she, doctor?"

"No doubt she is exquisite and flawless, but as lovely as she is, it looks like she's wearing a costume."

Miss Hudson snorted. "You prefer her in mismatched pyjamas and her hair mussed to high heaven?"

He didn't mean to speak so much, but the alcohol had loosened his lips. "I don't know if it's my place to say which I prefer her in. But there is no mistaking our Irene Holmes when she is having her morning tea in her robe and my slippers. No matter how much I try to hide them, she always finds them."

At the window, both Jeannie and Miss Carrington were fretting over Irene's bottom hem while she just rolled her eyes and let out a sigh.

Joe chuckled. "Oh, there she is."

He caught Miss Hudson smiling at him as if she knew some secret Joe had yet to share with anyone.

"Why are you looking at me like that?"

She took his arm. "I'm just glad our Irene found someone who accepts her for all her quirks."

"I'm sure her future husband will, too."

"Oh, I'm sure he will," the older woman said.

Joe's cheeks warmed all the way back to his ears. He gazed at his friend. Perhaps she didn't need a husband. And perhaps he didn't need a wife. Maybe they would just grow old together at Baker Street, solving the world's mysteries for the rest of their days.

Joe froze, assaulted by those thoughts. He glared at the glass of champagne, as if it was the drink's fault for such intrusive ideas.

Finally, Jeannie clapped her hands. "We are finished."

"Good," Irene said. Forgetting everything she'd just learned, she stomped toward the cart full of food.

Both women cried out, but it was the Madame who formed the warning. "Oh, no, you don't. I just did your nails and you are *not* messing this dress."

"But Jeannie," Irene whined, "I am *starved*."

"Fruit and biscuits only. And catch all the crumbs in your mouth."

Jeannie and Miss Carrington began tidying up as Miss Hudson broke the food into smaller pieces for Irene.

Joe watched with a grin on his face as she leaned forward, shoving some melon in her mouth. She grabbed a biscuit next, chewing stiffly. He couldn't help bursting into laughter. At the sound of his tipsy giggles, Irene started laughing too.

Jeannie came flying out of the bedroom and slapped Joe's shoulder. "Stop it, doctor. You'll crease her makeup."

"I am sorry," he stuttered, attempting to suppress the giggles. "It's just so ridiculous."

Miss Hudson slapped his other shoulder. "How would *you* like to put on the dress?"

Irene scoffed. "Oh, Miss Hudson. It *is* all so silly. Miss Carrington, I do admire you as this is all just too much."

The actress let out a light, feminine laugh. "I would gladly go through this rather than solve murders. It is I who admires you."

Irene continued snacking while Joe attempted yet another glass of champagne. While everyone else bustled about, he kept an eye on his friend. Her eyes darted around the room and her chewing became stiff and urgent.

She was getting nervous.

He was about to comfort her when the door opened to Mr. Barton. He paused, staring at Irene, then looked at Miss Carrington, then back.

"Marvellous! The car is here for you, Miss Holmes."

"I am Miss *Carrington*," she snapped. "Give me a moment. Everyone leave, I need to think and prepare."

Barton and Miss Carrington hesitated, but Jeannie and Miss Hudson, who knew Irene's process, scooted them out.

Joe set down his glass, but she snapped her fingers at him.

"Except you, Joe."

Miss Hudson patted him on the shoulder before making her own exit. The champagne had fogged up his head, but he tried to walk steadily over.

He needed some bread or heavy foods or else he wouldn't be near sober enough for this premiere. He'd been foolish to drink all that alcohol and Irene probably kept him back to scold him. The conversation between him and Sarah now felt like ages ago, but concern flashed in his gut, regardless. He shouldn't be drunk and alone with Irene – that was surely crossing boundaries, right?

But, as he stared at her, hands on her hips, taking short nervous breaths, he set his shoulders. His friend needed him.

Hang what everyone else thought. He snatched a couple of biscuits and a glass of water, and waited for her instructions.

Chapter VII

Catching a Killer at a Hollywood Premiere

Irene paced the room, attempting to stay upright in the high heels strapped to her feet. Her face was a mask of itself and she wanted to itch it off like mad. With all the poking and prodding, she'd managed to keep her nerves at bay for most of the day. But now, with the car ready, her stomach buzzed and her chest ached.

And she hated it.

"I am nervous, Joe." She kept pacing, shaking her hands, lest she ruin her nail polish.

Joe craned his neck back and forth, following her. "I'm not sure I've ever dealt with you nervous."

"The risk of this failing is two-fold. What if I can't play this part? I am not American, let alone an actress."

She spotted the half-glass of champagne in Joe's hand, swiping it from him. In two gulps, the bubbly alcohol was gone.

"Whoa, Irene. slow down."

He took the glass back and she put her hands on her hips. "I am in a dress that feels like it's barely on me, shoes that are too high to be sensible and my hair has never had so much product in it."

Irene had no idea how menacing she looked all dolled up, but the way Joe held the champagne glass out like a weapon to defend himself, she assumed she looked as intimidating as ever.

"You look—"

"I don't even have a brassiere on!"

It was inappropriate to mention such things in front of Joe, she knew, but she didn't care and it was not like he could do anything about her predicament, anyway. But venting her frustrations and worries was immensely satisfying. The champagne was settling very well in her stomach, so she decided on another. Aiming for the bar car behind Joe, she surged forward, but he caught her in a flash. He gently grabbed her waist and twirled her around. She stumbled into him but straightened quickly and set her shoulders, attempting a glare.

His cheeks were red, pupils dilated, but not from her comment about her brassiere. He'd had more than a few glasses of champagne. His shoulders were back and confident. The reflection of her gown glittered in his blue eyes. He clutched her hands in an attempt to calm her, but he spoke quick and excited.

"Miss Carrington is counting on us because she fears for her life. She needs our protection. We are the heroes tonight. *You are a hero.*"

"You're making us sound like we are in an American action film."

His face lit up. "Maybe we are! Maybe tonight you are the greatest action star in the world."

Her friend looked like he wanted to sing and dance and do a whole production. She had to admit; he looked quite spiffy in his bow-tie and black suit – the finest he'd ever looked, in fact. Though she wanted to share in his alcohol-filled excitement, her nerves still gnawed at her. "Then why do I not feel as glamorous as I should?"

Joe's gaze roamed over her face to her dress and back to her eyes as he sorted his words. She had no idea what she wanted him to say because she wasn't sure how she was even supposed to feel. A bit of apprehension was always normal when working undercover, but she never needed pep-talks or encouragement. Of course, the cases she'd worked before weren't nearly as exciting or elaborate.

He finally spoke. "I'm honestly not sure. Because you are pretending to be a real person? I don't know. But it doesn't matter. Your purpose for this is too great. And you are stunning. And confident. And are going to walk out there like you own this whole city, nay, the whole country! Ive seen you do it. Tonight, you are simply extra sparkly."

That speech got a laugh out of her, easing her nerves. Usually, she only needed Joe to calm her down or encourage her when she was nervous about her father. But this feeling of self-consciousness was new. Her friend pulled through like he always did.

He dropped her hands and spread his arms wide. "See? A smile that lights up the room."

She sighed at the dramatics, but her grin was still firmly planted on her face. "You are a hopeless romantic, Joe Watson."

He shuffled closer to her and gently cupped her face in his warm hands. "And you are Irene Holmes. You can do anything."

With her heels on, she was almost the same height as him. His bright eyes were nearly level with hers.

He was drunk, nervous, but had all the faith in the world in her.

Which meant she needed to have confidence in herself. She could let the world down, but she couldn't let Joe Watson down.

"You are correct. I am outstanding. I am amazing."

"Yes, you are."

He kept hold of her face and shuffled inches from her. A new nervousness took over her, and her heart rate rose as she felt the heat off of his body, so close to hers. It was a whole other distraction that simply wouldn't do. At least not at this time or place.

Where the right time and place was, Irene had no idea, but a part of her was curious to find out.

"If you so much as smudge one spec of make-up," she warned him, trying to halt this before more dangerous thoughts emerged. "Then Jeannie will have your head and I will be down a partner."

Joe dropped her face as if it were a hot potato and cleared his throat. "You're right. We should get going anyway."

He stepped away and took her by the arm toward the door.

* * * * *

A group of over fifty fans and at least a dozen reporters awaited Irene's arrival at the theatre. Joe sat beside her, occasionally patting her hand. The car stopped right in front of the red carpet. Fulfilling his duty, he hopped out and went around to open the door. Irene breathed deep, put on the face she'd been practising for the past twenty-four hours and emerged.

She kept her head lowered, grasping Joe's hand as she stepped onto the carpet. Mr. Radcliffe exited his own car behind them and hurried to her side. Together they started up the carpet, Joe following behind. The wind chilled her skin, but the evening was relatively warm compared to the past few days. Irene suddenly wished it wasn't so she could have the comfort of a luxurious fur throw around her bare shoulders.

Bulbs flashed in her face, people shouted. She had no idea where to look or who to smile at. Questions came at her as she tried her best to keep the grin plastered on her face.

"How are you feeling?"

"Are you still sick?"

"Is it serious?"

"Who was that man in the car with you?"

"Kathleen, look here!"

"Miss Carrington, over here!"

"Do you know anything about the posters being vandalised?"

Don's hand settled on her back as they walked. Though, normally, she abhorred such actions — unless it was Joe — Irene accepted his guidance if only because slapping it away would be out of character.

Before long, someone caught Don's attention and he stepped away from her. She froze for a second, mere yards from the door. A new hand touched her back as Joe took over, leading her into the building.

The noise level dropped dramatically, but there were still a few dozen people inside. Most of them were lined up, ready to greet her and Mr. Radcliffe. Irene paused for a brief moment and let Joe come right up to her back, his suit jacket brushing her dress.

Don finally caught up to them and did what he was supposed to. He intervened with anyone aiming for Irene, chatting and laughing, keeping the attention on himself as they made their way down the line.

A round man from the government extended his hand to her.

"Lovely to have you here, Miss Carrington."

She smiled just as she'd practised and mumbled in her best American accent. "Thank you."

The manager of the theatre also greeted them. "Miss Carrington, Mr. Radcliffe, what an honour it is hosting you. Please follow me."

Irene held her breath, waiting for the man to recognise her. But he appeared wholly bewitched by the two film stars.

As they followed him down the hall, she tried her best to study the staff working behind the scenes. There were so many people, yet none of them looked like they could be their suspect. She almost furrowed her brow in frustration, but kept her composure and entered the theatre room.

A quarter of the seats were already filled. More people filed in behind them. The manager led them to a row several forward from the one Joe claimed was the best for viewing. Irene settled in the seat between him and Don, letting out a sigh of relief. The hardest part was over. It should be all smooth-sailing from here. A confrontation with a murderer she could handle, but whatever happened back on that red carpet was something completely overwhelming and foreign to her.

She leaned to Joe. "I'd take a vile criminal over that any day."

He chuckled and whispered back, "I think it'd be different if you could be yourself and the questions were about crimes committed."

"Possibly, but I do not want to find out anytime soon."

She attempted to watch all the patrons that entered the room, but every time she made eye contact with someone, they'd wave enthusiastically, completely ruining her attempt to be subtle. Instead, she resigned to her seat and attempted to cross one leg over another, even though Miss Carrington had shown her how to sit with her heels delicately locked. Her dress, however, had other plans. The bottom flowed out, but it tapered at her knees and into her waist, meaning she had to twist the fabric to get her leg up. She must've been fidgeting more than she thought, because Joe put a hand firmly on her knee, keeping her leg down.

She finally gave in and folded her arms as the film credits started.

At about halfway through the picture, Irene tapped Joe's hand. Forty minutes should've been plenty of time to let the killer stew and fret about how they were going to get to "Miss Carrington" to kill her. Now, all Irene had to do was make an appearance and draw the murderer out.

She stood and slipped out of the row, avoiding the other patron's feet lest she trip and let out a very British swear word. Joe followed close behind, like the dutiful bodyguard he was. They pushed out into the lobby. She made a show of stretching and pulling attention toward herself.

A few employees wandered around, all staring and whispering. Hopefully, those got around to the right person. She started down the hallway to the lavatories, pausing before entering.

"Do not stand too closely. And do not stop anyone from entering the room. I want to catch her."

"You're smiling. You're about to confront a murderer and you're grinning like a fool."

"This is the fun bit."

Joe opened his mouth as if to give a stern warning, but then sighed and motioned behind her. "Go on, then."

Irene pushed on the heavy door into a small powder room. Her heels echoed loudly in the marble room; she immediately sat on the bench and slipped them off. Sighing at relief of having her flat feet on the cool floor, she dragged herself up and headed to the sink. It was like looking at a fun house mirror. Even though she looked like herself, she felt totally different. The crowd had got her on edge.

Closing her eyes, she breathed deep, smelling the marble and cleaning products. She only needed to be Miss Carrington for a short while more until the attacker revealed themselves.

Just then, the lavatory door flung open and a young woman walked in. Irene spun and assessed her. She'd seen her earlier, vaguely recollecting her standing next to an important-looking man.

This girl was barely fifteen years of age with arms like twigs. Not a killer.

"Oh, Miss Carrington! Do you mind if I powder my nose as well?"

Irene shook her head, then headed to the toilets. She stood next to the toilet bowl, very aware of her stockings and the nature of the room. She'd have to throw these out later.

She waited for the young girl to leave before returning to the mirrors. Her heart rate had settled to a steady beat. This was her forte: waiting for a murderer to walk through the door, not pretending to be someone else. Though, as the minutes dragged on, Irene thought that perhaps she'd made a mistake, that their suspect wouldn't follow her in here. Perhaps Joe was standing too close and had chased her off.

She decided to wait another moment, then if no one showed up, she'd pop out of the lavatory and do a round with the staff, with some excuse that she'd seen the film multiple times and simply couldn't watch herself again.

That would mean jumping back into her character, however, and she wasn't sure how much more of the actress she could pull off.

But she'd have to if she wanted her suspect.

A mere thirty seconds later, the door opened again.

A worker in overalls stepped in, her beady eyes searching the room. Her dirty blonde hair was frizzed and unkempt. She was shorter, stocky, with brawny arms and the march of someone seething with rage.

Irene calmed even more. Her plan worked.

The woman looked up at Irene. "Finally. It's actually you this time."

"Ominous," Irene said in her American accent.

The woman hesitated for a second.

Irene almost called to Joe. Maybe they could talk her down—

The woman let out a frustrated scream and charged forward, aiming her fist.

Irene sidestepped the blow and shoved the woman into the counter. She struck the back of her head with her elbow, yet she didn't go down. The suspect spun around, something gleaming in her hand.

A knife.

Standard issue army knife, to be precise.

Irene went for her wrist, but her assailant was fast. The blade slid across her arm, drawing a red line in her skin. She stumbled back, putting space between them. Miss Carrington's blasted dress was hampering her every step. She reached down and ripped the seam up to her thigh, then ran forward.

The woman threw a tray of napkins. Irene tried to dodge, but the ceramic hit her temple. She quickly shook her head and got her fists up.

She was ready for action.

Ready to end this case.

The enraged woman tried to swing again, but Irene caught and twisted her wrist. The knife landed with a clang on the marble, sliding across the room. The culprit grasped a handful of Irene's hair. They circled, both locked on to on another, crunching the shattered bowl beneath them.

The lavatory door flung open, distracting the woman. Irene twisted her arm. They both slipped on the broken bowl pieces and collapsed to the ground. Tiny pin pricks touched her thigh, ripping her stocking as she scrambled to her feet.

Free again, she immediately went for the knife across the room. She slipped on the shattered napkin holder and the sweat on the bottom of her feet, but got to the knife. She swiped the handle and turned.

Joe had the woman under the arms. She kicked her feet, lifting herself off the ground, thrashing around, screaming.

"Murderer! You killed him! Murderer!"

Beyond them, Don stood at the door to the lobby, eyes wide at the scene.

Irene yelled at him. "Get DI Lestrade. Now!"

He took off.

Joe struggled as the woman knocked them both backwards, but he had the height advantage. He spun her around, shoving her face against the wall.

With their target semi-subdued, Irene took a minute to catch her breath. Warm blood trickled down her leg. Something matted locks of hair to her temple, but she couldn't tell if it was sweat, or more blood. She wiped it away with her free hand.

Their suspect was bawling and heaving, hysterical, and Joe struggled to hang on to her.

Irene hurried beside him and pressed the blade to the woman's cheek. "Stop struggling and you might get out of here unharmed."

Chapter VIII

A Very Dangerous Delusion

Joe's arms strained as he held the woman against the wall. Even with a blade to the cheek, she still wriggled.

Lestrade tore into the room, followed by two constables and Radcliffe in tow. Joe waited until the constables had a good grip before releasing the suspect. She struggled against them too, but with both men dragging her away, there wasn't much to be done as they got her out of the lavatory.

Lestrade paused, pointed at Irene and addressed Joe, "Keep her here until I'm back."

"Then keep people away from this lavatory, or else they will get an eyeful," Irene snorted.

The DI gave a wave of acknowledgment and left.

With everything under control, Joe finally turned to his friend and felt himself pale. The long shallow slash on her arm bled slowly. There were a dozen tiny red cuts on her thigh, which was fully exposed. One of her dress straps had snapped, the fabric barely hanging on. He took off his jacket, slinging it carefully over her shoulders. He meant for it to simply sit there, but Irene stuck her arms through the sleeves.

He looked her up and down again, still holding the lapels of the jacket. "Are you alright?"

"Just scrapes. Well, this one hurts a bit."

He grasped her chin to look at the cut above her eye. "You're lucky."

"I'm skilled." She tried to wink, but winced instead.

Radcliffe circled them slowly, avoiding the broken ceramic pieces. "I've seen stunt men take fewer hits and go down. That was…"

Irene smirked as she tugged the jacket tighter around her. "That was my job."

Joe kept a protective arm around on her shoulders. The actor continued to ogle his friend as if he'd just seen the greatest action film on the planet.

Paying him no mind, Irene gazed down at the broken ceramic. "Real fights are never as clean or choreographed as in the pictures."

"She does this often?" he directed at Joe.

"More than I'd like."

Radcliffe's eyes drifted back to Irene's ripped seem before averting his gaze.

Joe's unease got the better of him. He guided Irene to a clean space on the floor, shifting her bare thigh away from Radcliffe.

Lestrade hurried back into the lavatory, aiming right for Irene. "You alright?"

"I am fine. Here." She extended her arm, dropping an army knife in Lestrade's hand.

"Another one? Where does she get them from?"

"The army supply shop across from the Renaissance Hotel," Joe said.

"Eddy," Irene said. "Do not interview that suspect until I am there."

"That woman is insane, Irene."

"Exactly. I intend to witness the interview as this is fascinating and a new, scary sort of violence to me." She shifted on her feet, putting more weight on Joe.

He held her up with ease, but knew she was hurting even more. She continued speaking, though, commanding the room as always.

"I cannot sneak out of here like this unless there is a clear path. So, here is the plan: Don is going to go back to the theatre and tell everyone that Miss Carrington was simply not feeling well and had to leave. Eddy, you are going to drive you car around to the back door and then make sure the coast is clear. Then Joe will escort me out. Now would be preferable, gentlemen."

Lestrade looked at Joe for assurance. He gave the DI a nod, sending him away. Radcliffe followed behind, but shot a final glance at them.

With the two men gone, Irene leaned even more on Joe and let out a pained sigh, dropping the bravado.

"You sure you're okay?"

"I did not mean to rip this dress so far up," she said with a chuckle. "But alas, anything for the case. Though, I don't know what shook Mr Radcliffe more: the fact that my knickers were showing or that you were unruffled by my appearance."

The image stuck out in his mind. The expensive silver dress torn right up Irene's leg, showing off strong but bruised muscles.

He cleared his throat but felt his ears warm. "It wouldn't do our cases very well if I got embarrassed by what you were wearing or showing."

She bumped him gently. "Your red face says different, but your willingness to try is all I ask."

He held her a little tighter, her slight frame tucking in nicely against his body, his fingers secure on her waist. The fabric of the dress was so thin that he felt every ridge of her ribs. Before he thought too much more about what his fingertips were touching, Lestrade came back into the room.

"I have cleaners here to get rid of this mess, as well as constables guarding it until the blood is at least gone. Let's get you out of here."

* * * * *

Within a half hour, Joe sat next to Miss Carrington on a sofa in her suite. Irene was busy in the bedroom, cleaning herself up. The fight at the theatre had sobered him up; he was now simply tired and hungry and ready for a cup of tea back at Baker Street.

His partner finally emerged, looking like herself again. She'd scrubbed her face and donned trousers and a shirt. She perched on a chair across from him while he studied the injury on her temple. Luckily, it didn't require a stitch, just a bandage to keep dust and dirt out while it healed. As he patched her cut, she spoke to Miss Carrington, her voice tired, and Joe knew she needed a cuppa as well.

"I will admit that this life is not for me. Too many people yelling and asking too many personal questions."

The actress laughed. "And yours is not for me. The studio would go crazy if I showed up with a cut on my face, let alone multiple bruises."

Irene smiled, crinkling Joe's bandage job. "Then we shall stick with our callings."

He wrapped a bandage around her arm, though the cut was shallow and had stopped bleeding within the hour. He stood to dispose of the rubbish and tissues. He couldn't help smiling as well as the women continued chatting. It was rare that Irene got on with anyone. He rarely witnessed a friendly conversation between her and others. She got along well enough with Sarah and her friends, but she'd dismiss them in a heartbeat.

This particular Irene was calm, tired, and genuinely friendly.

Miss Carrington sighed. "I truly do appreciate everything you've done. I don't quite understand it, but I am grateful for it."

Irene furrowed her brow.

Joe almost chided her for stretching the bandage again, then thought better of it.

"That woman thought you were the character you portray. She was convinced you'd killed her husband, and she was out to punish you."

"Oh, how sad. What will happen to her?"

Irene shrugged, then winced. "I'm not sure. If she lived in Britain, she'd be sentenced to jail, but with her being American, I do not know the procedure. I will be looking in on the interview, though, because all of this is fascinating."

"What is?"

"Someone living in delusion." Irene stood and paced, though she did so with a slight limp. "It's exceptionally intriguing to me how the human brain can ignore all reality and simply choose to believe something else, even though the obvious is right there."

The actress gave a light, tired laugh. "Well, Miss Holmes, we all do that to a degree."

"Yes, but we don't try to kill others. Now, we shall leave. I apologise that you had to miss your premiere."

Miss Carrington stood and glided forward with an outstretched hand. "Don't worry about it. I've been to dozens of premieres, and if I'm honest, a night in by myself was quite nice. I certainly would not have been as brave as you. Oh, and if you are ever in New York, please look me up. I know you would find the city fascinating."

Irene grasped her hand. "I certainly would. You will be the first person I contact if we ever visit."

Joe watched the whole interaction with a smile. It was so peaceful and nice after the fight at the theatre.

With the conversation now over, though, he pushed himself to his feet and wandered over to the actress, extending his own hand. "Safe travels back home."

"Thank you, Doctor."

By the time he was done saying goodbye, Irene was already at the door. Joe followed her out into the hall as she stifled a yawn. He held out his arm as they opted for the stairs.

"Are you sure you want to go all the way to Scotland Yard?"

"Of course. I want to see this through."

"Yes, but—"

Irene stopped on the pavement just outside the Vauxhall. "I need to see this interview, Joe. I need to see how far her delusion goes."

He knew there was no point arguing with her and that she would go downtown with or without him. He sighed and opened the passenger door to the car. "Fine, but I am driving."

"Joe, I…"

He stood firm with his choice and wiggled the door to make his point. She stared at him for a second longer, as he expected her to do, before climbing into the car and folding her arms in a pout.

* * * * *

The pair stood at the window, peering into the small interrogation room. The woman, who'd finally admitted her name was Leanne, was on the other side. Her overalls had small tears from the lavatory fight, and whatever the constables had to put her through to get her here in one piece. Her hair was frizzed, sticking up in every direction.

She struggled against the restraints as Lestrade paced in front of her. Two constables stood behind her, ready to grab her should she flail more.

Lestrade didn't get one word in before she shouted in a harsh American accent. "Let me go! I'm not a murderer. *She* is. Drag her in here and arrest her! I did you all a favour!"

"The woman you are referring to is an actress."

"She attacked me! She killed my husband!"

"And you killed two women."

She continued to shout and strain against the handcuffs.

Beside Joe, Irene shifted on her feet. She was eager to get into the room and throw her own questions at Leanne.

"I don't want you to go in there."

"I'll be fine, Joe."

He grasped her hands, holding firm. "She is in a completely different world. She may attack again. It took all my strength to hold her, so I'm worried she might rip right through those two boys."

Irene tried to tug free, but he held tight.

"I must get closer, Joe. Usually, the psychosis breaks once a person has been arrested, but she still truly believes the film is real."

"Exactly. We've come across dangerous people before, but nothing like this. Please, stay in here with me."

The image of her collapsed on the lavatory floor, leg cut up and bloody, flashed in his mind. He didn't need her more injured than she already was. He knew she wanted to learn everything she could about the conclusion of this case, about this new type of criminal, but he wouldn't let her sacrifice her safety for it.

Irene finally relaxed, slumping her shoulders and sighing.

"Thank you." He released her wrists.

The relief was short-lived. She launched herself out of the small room before he had a chance to react, slamming the door behind her.

Joe cussed but didn't go after her. The last thing the interview room needed was more people. He opened the door, though, ready to run out at a moment's notice.

Lestrade immediately went to argue with Irene as she stepped into the interrogation room, but she held up her hand.

The woman stopped shouting, her eyes glued to Irene and as wide as a dinner plate.

"You… Another lookalike? But you…"

"I was disguised as Miss Carrington. It was me you fought in the lavatory."

The woman looked her up and down, then recoiled in disgust. "Why? Why would you want to be her? If you only knew what she did…"

Irene sat in the chair across from her, calm and patient. Leanne huffed and writhed, looking extremely uncomfortable with the proximity, but Irene didn't budge.

"Tell me what she did. Perhaps I will change my mind and think her a foul woman, just as you do."

The woman glared at the three men standing around them, but started into her story. "My husband was a good man. Until *she* came along and poisoned him. Of course, I couldn't tell anyone, because everyone would think it's me. I had to bury his body in our backyard. I was so upset and I knew that she couldn't get away with it."

"Curious. And you are sure it was Miss Carrington that murdered your husband? And not Jane from the film 'The Thief At Midnight'?"

Leanne nodded furiously. "Jane! Yes, that was her name. She was clever, using an alibi to travel."

"Kathleen Carrington is the alibi?"

"Yes."

"And you followed her all the way from America to seek revenge?"

Leanne nodded.

"And you didn't think to come to the police?"

"The police? What would they do? They'd just think I was crazy. They would lock me up and my husband would be just another victim to that horrendous woman."

Joe couldn't quite believe what he was hearing. This woman truly needed help. Would Irene be gentle enough not to rile her up?

His friend regraded Leanne, but the woman spoke before she could get another word in. "So many of you Brits look like her that it took me a few tries—"

"A few murders," Irene interjected.

Leanne scoffed. "They weren't Jane. They weren't important. *She* is still out there, walking around, laughing as if she didn't poison my husband. He deserves justice."

"Have you seen the film 'The Thief at Midnight'?"

"I've seen lots of films. I tend to see them by myself—"

"After you and your husband fight. To clear your head and to escape the horrors of what had occurred."

Leanne grew nervous, shifting in her chair. "Horrors? I don't know what you mean."

"Your husband hits you, then you go see a film to pretend it never happened."

This comment clearly caught Leanne off guard and she stumbled through her words before settling on an answer. "My husband did no such thing."

Irene stood, folding her arms. "You are covered in old wounds. The two fingers on your left hand were broken a few years ago and were never set properly. Your face is slightly lopsided as if a bone had been cracked as a result of a black eye. Every time one of those constables makes a sudden move, you flinch. You went into hysterics when my male colleague attempted to subdue you in the lavatory, the act obviously dredging up something unpleasant. Also, I do not believe one simply has a psychotic break without prompting. You had a nasty row with your husband, to which he hurt you fairly badly, and then you went to the pictures. You saw the film and conjured up a delusion in which your husband was poisoned. Then, you carried out that plan on your own – no help from a woman named Jane – but your mind ran away with itself even more as the horror of what you'd done set in. The guilt set in. Revenge was in your brain, and though you'd just carried out revenge for yourself against an abusive husband, your delusions convinced you that you wanted revenge *for* him."

Leanne's face turned a bright red. "No. That's not... My husband was a good... *She* killed him. Not me. *She* did!"

"She did not."

The woman grew louder and strained against the cuffs. "I didn't kill him, you stupid bitch. *She* did. I loved my husband. I didn't kill him!"

Joe needed to get Irene out of there before she caused this woman to have a heart attack. Plus, his stomach turned at this tale and he needed to step away himself.

As he entered the small room, Lestrade had already stepped between the two women. He guided Irene to Joe, who grasped his friend's arm yet again.

"The hallway," Lestrade said. "Now."

Irene followed easy enough. Soon the three of them were in the narrow brick hallway. Joe released her, but blocked the access to the interview room, lest she get the idea to burst back in there.

Lestrade, who looked as exhausted as Joe felt, rubbed his face. "That story you told—"

"That was no story. It was the truth. I'm sure her husband beating her is what caused the break. She reacted and has carried out a delusion. Find out where she lives and ring the police there. She's murdered and buried her husband."

Inside the room, Leanne was sobbing and calling out a man's name. Lestrade glanced at the room, but Irene ignored the sounds as she paced, still limping.

"It's as if her brain is simply refusing to acknowledge what happened. It is all so fascinating. Oh, I wish I'd studied psychology more. Can I go back in there and—"

"No." Both Joe and Lestrade spoke in unison.

She scowled at them.

Lestrade patted her shoulders. "Right now, you need to go home. There isn't anything more you can do for her. But, know you are in our debt for luring her to the lavatory to be caught."

"I am in your debt for a lot of things, dear Eddy."

He kissed her cheek. "Well, at least your head hasn't grown from the flattery."

"Good night and good luck," Joe said. "Do let us know how this all wraps up?"

"Certainly."

He thought for a moment that Irene wouldn't follow him with how her gaze was fixated on the interview room. But he held out his arm, knowing she always grasped it whenever offered. It had become a Pavlovian response by this point.

True to form, she slipped her arm in his and they headed home.

While he would miss The Ritz and all its glamour, he was glad this case was over. Not only had it been particularly violent, but it forced him to feel certain things he wasn't ready to face yet, both with Sarah and Irene.

He couldn't wait to sleep on his bumpy mattress and dream about getting a bed as comfortable as The Ritz.

Chapter IX
Home Sweet Home

The following evening saw the end of this horrid case. Leanne was on her way back to America where she would be detained at a psychiatric hospital for the criminally insane.

Meanwhile, the cinema manager gave them free rein for any film they wanted to see for the rest of the year, much to Joe's delight. Irene even admitted to being a *bit* chuffed to watch more films, though deep down, she was more excited than she let on.

As for the actors, Miss Carrington and Mr. Radcliffe had one more night in London. Kathleen was to make a special appearance to take photos and sign autographs for the fans she missed at the premiere, all under the guise that she'd been ill.

Joe took Sarah to "The Thief at Midnight", though he lamented to Irene that a break from the cinema would've been nice, for just a short while. He'd left with a funny expression on his face that Irene couldn't quite place. A bit of apprehension and exhaustion, perhaps? She didn't dwell on it too long, because she left just minutes after him.

As promised, now that the case was finished, she went to visit Don Radcliffe in his suite. He beckoned her in and started pouring her a drink immediately. He'd dressed casually, in slacks and a button-up shirt, but the scent of his signature expensive cologne floated throughout the room. They chatted about nothing in particular as he poured his own drink before handing her a glass.

Irene perched on the sofa in the sitting area, expecting him to sit across from her. Instead, Don sat next to her, leaned back and relaxed, arm outstretched.

"I thought I wouldn't get you over here," he said. "Especially after getting to know Doctor Watson."

Irene sipped her drink and the strong spirits warmed her down to her toes. Perhaps she should have a drink after every case; it certainly agreed with her body.

"What does Joe have to do with it?"

"He's very protective of you."

"He does not control me."

"Oh good lord, no. And he knows it. But, the man is practically in love with you."

This drew a laugh from her. "You are mistaken, Mr. Radcliffe. We're good friends and partners. What you see is friendship, familiarity, and protectiveness."

The actor took another sip of his drink, but there was a playfulness in his eyes.

She was being cautious, but really had no other motive than the fact that she was curious; she wanted to see if she could best his ego. Though, the way his dark eyes moved across her gave her an odd butterfly feeling.

"You strike me as someone who doesn't watch a lot of films," he said.

"I do not."

"Not even 'A Trip To El Paso'? That was everywhere last year. I learned to ride a horse and fight on horseback."

She snorted and took a few bigger sips of her drink. "Not an unusual skill. My partner can do that too. And as for fighting, you'd impress me if you could do it in a gown and heels."

Don laughed, the sound more pleasant than Irene thought it would be. "Well, you got me there."

"Also, I find I can often predict the end not even halfway through."

"I still find it very intriguing how unimpressed you are with me. You didn't even dress up."

She lifted her leg. "These are my finest trousers! Besides, if you were a gentleman and taking me out somewhere nice, I would've attempted. But as it is, we are simply sitting in your hotel room."

He regarded her with narrowed, curious eyes, then set his drink down. "Stand up. I want to show you something."

He strolled over to the large window. Peeling back the curtains, he stepped back to give her space. Irene had no idea what he was playing at as she'd seen out a window before, but she decided to humour him.

Outside, pitch black had settled over the city, but the lights of London shone brightly. It caught her off guard. This view looked toward Baker Street, and though there were a million lights, she swore she could see 221b's sitting room lamp on.

She almost forgot where she was and who she was with until she caught movement in her peripherals.

"Look at that," she said. "You've finally impressed me."

Don shuffled closer to her, and she caught a whiff of dark, rich cologne and even richer alcohol. He pushed a stray curl from her face. "Maybe there's more I can do to impress you."

His finger traced a gentle line down her cheek as his gaze dropped to her lips.

* * * * *

She arrived home a little over an hour later, humming some song she heard Miss Hudson sing in the kitchen. Before she could put a foot on the step, the very same lady came out from her flat.

"Where have you been?" Her ever-scrutinising eyes narrowed.

"Out for a walk. Enjoying the pleasant evening." She started up the stairs, but that didn't stop Miss Hudson from calling after her.

"I'm curious to know how a stroll around the neighbourhood could smudge your lipstick like that."

Irene should've kept jogging upstairs. Instead, she whirled around and was met with a wry smile from the older woman.

"But it's none of my business. Until it is, of course."

"It is none of your business, period."

Miss Hudson kept the smirk on her face as she sauntered into her flat.

* * * * *

Another hour later, Irene sat on the couch in fresh pyjamas and two of Joe's mismatched slippers. She'd forwent the curlers, letting her damp hair tumble around her shoulders.

Joe arrived home and shrugged off his jacket, kicked off his shoes, then flopped into his chair across from her.

"How was the third viewing of the picture?" she asked.

He laughed. "Predictable. How was your evening?"

"Pleasant."

"Oh, well, that's good then!"

She hadn't told him that she was going to visit Don at the hotel and, for some reason, she felt the need to keep it from him now. It sat a bit sour in her stomach. She'd never kept something like this from Joe. Anecdotes from her past, yes, but never anything in the present. As Irene stared at him, tired and slightly dishevelled, she almost started to speak.

This was Joe. Her friend. Her confidant.

He could handle a story of how she'd spent her evening, right?

But before she could open her mouth, he stood. "I'm going to get changed for the evening. Then I very much look forward to a cuppa by the fire because this week has been a long one."

Ten minutes later, he sat across from her again, in his robe and the matching mismatched pair of slippers.

Miss Hudson showed up with late-night tea and lingered an extra moment. She raised a brow at Irene, then glanced at Joe. Irene looked between the two but couldn't begin to fathom what the landlady meant by her actions. So, she ignored her.

Miss Hudson rolled her eyes and left the room.

As the pair sipped their tea, Irene's mind drifted to films and stories, then to her uncle and the cases he'd recorded about her father. A thought came to her that was almost too absurd to say out loud.

"Joe… Do you think anyone else has written about my father? Like stories from their own brain? Made up cases for their own amusement?"

Her partner considered her, pursing his lips in thought. "Perhaps? I'd say… probably?"

"What do you think they've written?"

"I have no idea, Irene. Your father solved some very unique cases. It would take a creative mind to come up with the same type."

Her ribs tightened over her lungs, but she stayed calm as she stared at the floor. Joe leaned forward in his chair. His gentle coaxing got the better of her and she spoke what was on her mind.

"I know every title of the stories Uncle John wrote, but I've never read a single one. A quarter of them were written after I was born."

"Really? But you're not mentioned in any story."

She looked at him, a new panic starting up. "You've read them?"

His face reddened. "Uh, well, I started them a few weeks ago. Miss Hudson was mending my trousers and I saw her collection sitting there. I started to read while waiting for her to finish. I'm sorry, Irene, I should've told you."

To her surprise, she didn't care that he'd read them and kept it from her. Joe was a reader and, just like her and her cases, if a book was laid in front of him, he'd investigate it.

She was concerned about something else, though.

"Are the stories good?"

He gave her a soft smile that crinkled his eyes. "They're very good. Your uncle had a certain way with words that make the stories wholly engaging."

"How many have you read?" Her words came out stiffer than she meant. In reality, she was surprisingly calm and genuinely curious to know more. How long would that curiosity last, she had no idea. But, for now, she would run with it, if only because she knew she was on the brink of shutting down.

His smile dropped, nervous again. "They were so good that I kept reading them. I'm up to about a dozen."

A little voice inside her was telling her to stop asking questions as it would only lead to more anxiety. But Irene shoved those thoughts away. She wasn't scared or nervous, she decided. This was simply her body's automatic response, as it had been for years when discussing Father and Uncle John. But she wanted to change that.

And tonight she had a chance.

"What's your favourite story so far?"

Joe sat back and thought for a moment, chuckling. "I quite enjoyed The Solitary Cyclist."

"What was he like in that one?"

"He sent your poor uncle out to the countryside by himself, chided him for failing to bring back useful information, then proceeded to travel out there on his own and get into a boxing match with a bar patron. It very well could've been me and you in that exact same scenario. Although, I am grateful that you don't send me off on my own nearly as often as your father sent your uncle. But you most definitely take after him, stubbornness and all." He paused and thought for a moment. "Perhaps that's why I was so keen on reading more stories. There was a comfort to them. A familiarity. Like reading stories about our own adventures."

Irene grinned as she thought of what poor Uncle John endured because he'd failed to grasp some concept that Father was twenty steps ahead in.

She was so damn curious about the stories, but she had yet to summon the courage to pick them up. She knew it would crush her to imagine her father at the peak of his life, running around London, solving crimes. Irene's heart was fragile enough these days – certainly since the war – that she couldn't afford any distractions.

Unless she didn't have to read them on her own.

"Perhaps…" Her words caught in her throat. She cursed and tried again. "Perhaps, one day you can read me one?"

"I'd love to."

Joe's lilting northern accent may keep some of the hurt at bay. At least, that was her theory. She'd hear her friend's tone and cadence, rather than her father's voice.

A year ago, Irene would've never considered even speaking about her uncle's stories. She'd even gone to great lengths to keep her lineage hidden. Now, she was accepting having the tales not just sitting out in the living room, but being read to her.

She knew it would still take some time to write that letter to her father that everyone wanted her to; if only she could force these negative, sad feelings away. But, alas, she kept having to work through them. It was painful and silly, and she hated it.

Her eyes watered and she cussed. She stared at the floor, hoping to dispel the waterworks before a traitorous tear ran down her cheek. She felt the cushions next to her sink as Joe's tall body folded itself on the couch. He wrapped his arm around her and tugged her close.

"You're doing well, Irene. There is no timeline for these sorts of things. You've come leaps and bounds since last year."

She nodded, rubbing her face in his robe. "I would still like to get to the point where I don't cry when I speak about him."

"That may never happen, but it doesn't mean you haven't moved forward."

They sat in silence for half a minute before she felt Joe's belly move in laughter.

"It does give me some comfort, knowing your poor uncle had to endure the same stress you give me. Though how he handled both your father *and* you is well beyond me."

Irene laughed as images of Uncle John's scowl filled her mind. She had too many memories of his chiding and exasperated sighs.

"His hair did grey quite early on."

"I can only imagine."

Joe rubbed his thumb on her arm in a soft, soothing rhythm that instantly comforted her. Her eyelashes began to droop, but she perked up again when he spoke:

"You should be proud of yourself, Irene. I'm certainly proud of you."

She smiled again; the compliment warming her down to her toes. She was proud of herself too, if only for finally feeling normal again.

She stayed tucked up into Joe, taking comfort in his closeness. His strong hands were delicate and light. His thumb continued to stroke her bicep. He smelled like lemon and tea and the richness of 221b.

A small stirring started in her stomach, not unlike the flapping that accosted her when she'd been with Mr. Radcliffe earlier in the evening. Irene had only felt these butterflies a few times before, but they were becoming more frequent. This time, they were accompanied by a hearth heating her from within.

A part of her wanted to stay on this couch forever and say 'bugger off' to anyone who would interrupt them. Another was concerned with the comparison to her time with Don. Joe was very different from a suave American actor charming her in his hotel room. Yet, why did it elicit the same feelings?

Panic set in as she begun to overanalyse her body's reactions. Irene swept all thoughts of warmth and Joe away with a violent swing of a broom. She would not even entertain such silly ideas, concocting scenarios about feelings that were or weren't there.

She did, however, need to go to sleep.

"I'm off to bed now."

Joe nodded, but kept his arm draped over her. "I am back at the vet practice tomorrow, but I shall try to be as quiet as I can when I leave in the morning."

His hand slid down her arm as she stood and he interlocked their fingers, as if not wanting to let her go. Irene humoured him and stood still for a brief second.

"Goodnight, Joe," she whispered.

He squeezed her hand before releasing her. "Goodnight, Irene."

She wandered to her bedroom, but glanced back at her friend. He hadn't moved from the couch; instead he stared at the ground, eyes in a haze. He was rubbing together the fingers that had grasped hers.

Irene had no idea what was running through his mind, but he was most likely overthinking. And he was exhausted.

She shut her bedroom door quietly. Instead of heading for her bed, she dragged a large, flat trunk to the centre of the carpet. The lock was simply for show and she popped it off with ease. Amongst photographs and precious objects from her childhood were a set of the first edition of Uncle John's stories. She reached out to touch the spine, but recoiled.

She was so close, but pulling out the stories simply wasn't in the cards for tonight. And that was okay, according to Joe. There was no timeline. Though she wished there was. Then she could calculate just how far along she'd come, and the distance she still needed to travel.

She shut the lid and slid the trunk back to its place in the corner under an ever-growing pile of laundry.

Perhaps she should keep a diary of her own adventures? She snorted, knowing the whole thing would dissolve into scribbles on napkins.

Yawning, she dived under sheets that were much too thin. She rolled over on a mattress that could use an upgrade.

Horns honked from outside the small window. Joe and Isla thumped around upstairs. The old pipes in the wall creaked.

221b was definitely not The Ritz, but it was home and it, along with the people she shared it with, suited her just fine.

THE END

HOLMES & CO. WILL RETURN IN:

THE ADVENTURES OF HOLMES & CO. PART II

About the Author

 Allison Osborne lives in Ontario, Canada with her son, their West Highland terrier, and an overwhelming amount of vintage trinkets. She attended the University of Western Ontario for creative writing, and when her mind isn't wandering through 1940s England, she's busy dabbling in scriptwriting and other grand adventures.

Connect with Allison

Instagram: @allisonoauthor
Web: www.aosborneauthor.com

Milton Keynes UK
Ingram Content Group UK Ltd.
UKHW020339040624
443602UK00010B/139